My Colorblind Rainbow

By Chanel Hardy

More Acknowledgements

THANK YOU TO EVERYONE who has ever shared or liked a post, bought a book, or downloaded it even if you haven't read it yet.

Thank you to Asha Fields, my friend and beta reader who was one of the first to ever read this story, back when it was a mess in its baby stages.

Thank you to Big Black Chapters, a group of some of the most encouraging Black writers and readers I have ever known.

Thank you to my wonderful husband, for finally cleaning out the storage closet and encouraging me to finish this story.

Thank you to my mother and sisters for always hyping me up on social media!

Thank you to Sabrina Carnesi, for being such a huge fan of MCR and getting my work acknowledged on In The Margins Award lists.

Thank you to all of my LGBTQA friends for being amazing, brave individuals who inspire me to be more open about my own feelings and to not put myself in a box or attach my sexuality to any labels.

And last but not least, thank YOU.

Chapter 1

NORTH CAROLINA, 1940

"I hate you!" fifteen-year-old Darlene Jones screamed, ruffling her hair after a boy in her class teased her. He thought it would be funny to put a worm in her hair and watch her squirm like a five-year-old girl, which she did, but she didn't find it funny at all. She hated nasty, crawly things just as much as she hated stupid games played by immature boys.

"Girl, you know they're just playing!" Janet fixed Darlene's ponytail, attempting to comfort her best friend. "It's just a worm!"

"Whatever."

Janet and Darlene had known each other since Darlene moved down south from New York. They were inseparable, but sometimes Darlene couldn't help but feel like Janet didn't understand her. Darlene often felt that way about everyone around her. That nobody understood her. She didn't even understand herself, sometimes.

"I just don't get them." Darlene expressed in frustration.

"Huh?"

"Boys. I don't get boys sometimes. They annoy me so much."

Janet scoffed at Darlene. "Well, I don't get you sometimes, always so serious. It was just a joke."

Darlene shrugged. Although she knew her friend was only kidding, she didn't care for her comment. "I guess so. Anyways, you want to hang out for a little while before you go home?"

"Okay. I've got to stop by the Rosenberg's store to get some bread for my mama first."

Muriel and Christopher Rosenberg were a Jewish mother and son who ran the local store in town. Unlike typical southern bigots, they were a nice family. As the girls walked inside the dusty store, the loud bell attached to the top of the door jingled to the merchants of customers. Mrs. Muriel was behind the counter handling a customer, while her son was stocking a few shelves with medicines—Muriel's homemade remedies. A thin, eighteen-year-old with thick dark hair and round glasses, Christopher moved his curly hair out of his face, as he became distracted when Darlene walked in. Every time she came by the store, it made his day. He was an antisocial young man, never having more than a few words of small talk with anyone but would muster enough courage to say hello to Darlene. He'd had a crush on her for some time now, but knew he had no chance of pursuing a girl like her. He smiled and greeted Darlene as usual.

"Hey, Darlene," he shoved his hands in his pant pockets, "and Janet. Can I help you girls today?"

"No thank you, Christopher. We're just here to get some bread. It's nice to see you." Darlene smiled and continued walking past him.

"Did you see that?" Janet teased, poking Darlene's shoulder.

"See what?"

"Every time you come in here, Christopher is always smiling at you. I think he likes you," Janet teased, still poking her.

"What?" She jerked her shoulder. "Stop poking me. No. He's just being nice. Besides, my daddy would throw a fit. That's not going to happen."

Although she had no romantic interest in Christopher, the thought of labeling herself as something less than him because of the color of her skin wasn't something she took well. It also didn't help that Blacks, especially in the south, enabled that idea by being so apprehensive whenever Whites were around. She and Janet went up to the counter to pay for the bread.

"Hello, girls! You look nice today!" Mrs. Rosenberg greeted.

Muriel was a plump woman, with big hair as dark and curly as her son's. Mr. Rosenberg passed away a few months earlier. Despite his passing, Muriel had such a positive attitude and a polite smile. Darlene knew how it felt to lose a loved one. Her mother died when she was eight years old, leaving Darlene behind with her father, Joe Jones, Grandmother Anne, and older brother Darren. They moved to Durham, North Carolina, a year before her mother passed. It was nice, but not like New York.

"Thank you, Mrs. Rosenberg," the girls replied in unison, leaving the store, heading toward Darlene's house.

As they walked toward the porch, Darlene's dad came out the house, marching toward his daughter, as if he was going off to war.

"Girl! Where were you? You know I don't like to worry!" He yelled.

"Sorry, Daddy, we made a stop, so Janet could get some bread for her mama."

Guilt blanketed her father's face. Since his wife died, he became ex-tra protective over his children. He was a hardworking man, a chauffeur for a rich White family who lived near town.

His stiff posture relaxed. "It's okay, baby girl. You know I just don't like to worry. You kids are all I got." He pulled her into him and hugged his daughter.

Breaking their embrace, Darlene asked, "Is it okay if Janet stays for a while?"

"Of course, baby. Just not too late," he warned.

The girls rolled their eyes and replied, "We know," with a hint of at-titude, as they headed inside the house and to Darlene's room.

Darlene's brother, Darren, was in his room, working on his home-work.

"Hey, Darren!" Janet waved with a cute smile. She always flirted with Darren, most girls did. But he always brushed it off.

"Hi, Janet." He was not at all amused by her attempt to be flirty.

"Your brother is so cute!"

Darlene made a gagging gesture toward Janet in a humorous man-ner. Not only did she hate thinking of her brother in that way, but she also didn't want to think about boys at all. Other than her brother, father, and friend Walter, she didn't find being around the opposite sex entertaining at all.

They were often boring and unpleasant.

"You want to do my hair?" Janet asked.

Janet had long, soft, dark brown curly hair. The kind most girls like Darlene wished they had. It felt like feathers and bounced back each time you pulled out a curl. She could do whatever she wanted with it. Janet's grandmother was a White woman, which was where she got her nice hair texture. Janet never knew much about her grandmother. Her mother was abandoned as a child and didn't like to talk about her. Janet's mom, Mary Benson, raised her daughter alone, so Janet didn't have much of a family growing up. Darlene's family was the closest thing to a real family she had.

"I wish I had hair like you," Darlene said, unraveling Janet's braids.

"Why? You have pretty hair, too."

Darlene had a rougher hair texture, full of naps and coils. She couldn't do much with it, but tie it back into a ponytail, unless Grandma Anne braided it for her. Rough, dry, and unmanageable, she sometimes wore her hair down if the weather allowed, which was hard living in the south with humid summers.

"I hate my hair. It's too thick." Darlene picked at a strand of her hair.

"You hate everything, girl—boys, your hair, having fun. What do you like?"

"I do not hate everything! That's not true!" Darlene shoved Janet on the shoulder in a playful manner.

Darlene often wondered about herself. She knew she was different, but never quite understood why.

"I... like you," she replied with a soft tone in her voice as she ran her fingers through Janet's soft hair. "I mean, I like you because you're my best friend. My only friend, really."

"You're my best friend, too Darlene."

The girls shared a quick moment of silence and smiles. "So," Janet said with emphasis, "what about Christopher?" She teased.

"What about him? I told you he doesn't like me, and I don't like him, anyway." Darlene was becoming annoyed with the subject of Christopher. It was getting old, and she wanted to skip the subject. "I think we should get started on our homework soon."

• • ൸ • •

THE NEXT MORNING, DARLENE got up a little early for school. Grandma Anne was in the kitchen making pancakes. She always made her special pancakes on Friday. Darlene never knew what was so special about her grandma's pancakes, but a part of her didn't want to know. After Darlene and Darren's mother died, Grandma Anne made pancakes every morning for a month to help them cope with the loss.

Darlene once asked her grandma, "What's so special about your pancakes?"

"Honey, let me tell you something." Her grandmother began. "If you enjoy it, and it makes you happy, then you don't need to ask questions. Just enjoy it while you can because the things you love the most can be gone in the blink of an eye."

Darlene thought of her memories with her mother every time she thought about her grandmother's words. Since that day, those words stuck with her, and she tried to apply them to her everyday life of living in the moment. She grabbed her plate of pancakes and pulled up a seat at the table.

"I'm glad you made this today, Grandma. I needed this." Said Darlene, taking a bite out of her food.

"What's going on, baby?"

"Nothing, really, just stupid boys at school."

"Well, what did they do to you?"

"They played a stupid joke on me. I know it was just for fun, but I hate it when boys do stupid things. I hate boys!" Her father overheard her as he entered the kitchen.

"Whoa now, sweetie! I don't want to hear my baby girl talking like that!"

Darren followed their father into the kitchen. "Yeah, what do you like, girls or something?" he teased and laughed.

Appalled and angry, Joe twirled around and slapped Darren across the face. Stunned, Darren's eyebrows shot up in surprise and his mouth gaped open, as he stumbled backwards, grabbing the side of his face.

Between clenched teeth, Joe spewed, "Don't you ever let me hear you say any of the devil's foolishness like that again, boy! You hear me?"

Darlene and Grandma Anne jumped, startled by Joe's sudden outburst.

"Jesus Christ, Joe! Don't hit the boy like that!"

Darren noted his father's set face, his clamped mouth and fixed eyes and muscle flicked angrily in his haw. "I'm sorry, Dad." Darren's bottom lip quivered, as he held back tears.

Although Darlene felt embarrassed by her brother's comment, she was sure her brother felt worse. The family spent the rest of breakfast in silence.

During her walk to school, Darlene couldn't help but think about her brother's comments. *Why would he say that? Me? Like girls? How stupid!*

Darlene walked into the classroom and found a seat next to Walter Smith, who was tall, dark, and looked much older than the other kids due to his height.

"Hey, Darlene!"

"Hey, Walter." She wasn't in the mood for her friend's conversation.

"What's wrong? You look sad."

"Nothing. Just tired." She didn't want to tell anyone about what happened at breakfast.

. . ❧ . .

"WHO WANTS TO GO FIRST and present their book report to the class?" Mrs. Fontaine, the teacher, stood up behind her desk and faced the class.

"Oh! Me!" Emily yelled out from the opposite end of the room. "I want to go first, Mrs. Fontaine!"

Emily Carter was one of the pretty girls. The boys liked her, and the girls wanted to be her, except Darlene and Janet. Darlene was far more comfortable being an outcast, than associating with the likes of Emily and her bourgeois attitude.

Emily was repulsively vain and carried herself as if she was better than everyone and everything. Darlene and Janet couldn't understand how she had any friends at all. Emily pranced to the front of the class-room, swinging her long, smooth hair.

She was one of the lighter girls, with creamy skin, feathery hair like Janet's. Emily came from interracial parents—a White father and Black mother—so her mixed features were more prominent than Janet's. While Emily read her report, Darlene gazed out the window to her left, distracted as usual, and hoping Mrs. Fontaine would call on her last. She thought about what happened at breakfast that morning with her father and brother. It had her feeling uneasy all day; not so much her father's reaction to Darren's comment, but the comment itself.

After school, as Darlene and Janet were walking home, Emily caught up with them and approached Darlene.

"Hey, Darlene, we're friends, right?" Emily asked with a hint of smug.

With a confused expression, Darlene shrugged. "Umm, sure."

"Great! I was wondering if you could talk to your brother for me. I think he's really cute!"

Darlene knew Darren would have no interest in Emily. He was two years older and too mature to entertain a girl like her.

"Umm, yeah. Okay, I will." Darlene lied.

"Thanks, hun!" Emily ran to catch up with her friends and then turned around. "Oh, Darlene!"

"Yeah?"

Emily and her friends giggled. "Nice hand-me-down skirt! My maid has one just like it."

Emily was mean, making fun of her old, wool skirt that was a hand-me-down from Grandma Anne's younger years, but Darlene ignored her.

"Oh forget her! Nobody likes Emily anyway. They just pretend to. Bunch of fools." Janet hugged Darlene.

Darlene smiled. Janet was a good friend to her. She was smart, kind, and beautiful, a girl any boy would be lucky to have.

When Darlene got home, she tossed her books on her bed, and walked out to the porch where her grandmother was sitting and sat on the chair next to her.

"Grandma Anne, can I ask you a question?"

"Sure, baby."

"Why did Daddy get so angry at Darren this morning?" "Well, baby, your brother said something he had no business saying."

She looked at her grandmother. "Can I ask you something else?"

"Sure, baby."

"Why is it a bad thing? Race mixing, girls liking girls, or boys liking boys? I mean, I know God says we're supposed to be man and woman and race mixing isn't right, but why is it a sin? Shouldn't God love His children anyway?"

Grandma Anne's face held a questionable look. "Well, can I ask why you want to know so badly, little girl?"

Darlene was embarrassed, again. "Just asking, Grandma."

"Well, you should know better than to question God's ways."

Darlene got up from the chair. "I'm going to go get started on my homework. Love you, Grandma."

"Love you, too, baby."

Later that night, Darlene sat on the edge of her bed, holding a little flowerpot, with one daisy. She held it up to her nose, taking in the sweet aroma. Grandma Anne had given her seeds to plant and, after keeping it at the window in the front of the house for months, it sprouted.

Her father entered her room. "Can we talk, sweetie?"

He piqued her curiosity. "Okay, Daddy. What's wrong?"

"Your grandmother tells me you're curious about things."

Darlene felt an instant nervous pain in her stomach. She felt betrayed.

"About what, Daddy?"

Joe paused. "Have you been doing anything with that Rosenberg boy?"

"Christopher? Of course not, Daddy. We're just friends, I guess. I barely know him that well."

"Good. Because you know that's not right. You can't go around messing with these White boys. You're a good Christian girl. You know better."

Darlene was fighting back the urge to squeal at him. She was more irritated than upset with the idea that everyone seemed to think she had any interest in Christopher. Or, that he had any interest in her.

"Okay, Daddy. Nothing's going on, I promise." She was ready to end the conversation. "How was work today, Daddy?" She wanted to skip the awkward subject of her love life.

"It was okay. Mr. Caldwell wasn't in too much of a bad mood today."

The Caldwell family was a White rich family that lived in the northern part of Durham. Darlene didn't know too much about the family her father worked for, except that some days he came home in a good mood and a bad mood other day. The days he came home angry, Darren and Darlene tried their best to stay out of his way.

"Get some sleep, baby girl. You've got school tomorrow." He kissed her forehead and left her room.

Darlene didn't know what to feel, but she knew breakfast would be awkward the next morning.

Chapter 2

"TURN THAT NOISE OFF, Rose and come to dinner, please!" Mrs. Caldwell yelled upstairs from the dining room.

Stretched out across her bed, nineteen-year-old Rose Caldwell smashed out her cigarette and turned off her record player. She had been listening to "When the Saints Go Marching In" by Louis Armstrong. It was her favorite song. Listening to music was her escape from her humdrum reality.

She made her way downstairs to join her parents for dinner, singing along with the song still playing in her head.

She walked into the dining room. Her parents, Albert and Barbara Caldwell, sat at the table. Their servant, May, an older Black woman, who had been working for the Caldwell family since Rose was two years old, handed Rose her plate.

"Thank you, May." Rose said politely.

"You don't have to be extra polite to May, she's doing her job," her father said.

"I know that, Father, but she's still a person and I treat her like one."

Brought up in a wealthy family like most of her peers, Rose was different. In more ways than anyone ever knew. Her father gave her a look of annoyance by every sentence that came out of her mouth. Her mother broke the awkward silence.

"Have you been smoking again?"

"No, Mom!" She sighed heavily. The annoyance was beginning.

Mrs. Caldwell smiled in exasperation. "Honey, why don't you grow your hair back? It was so beautiful."

"Because, Mom, I like my hair like this."

It annoyed Rose when the subject of her appearance came up, especially her hair. She had beautiful red hair that went perfect with her bold gray eyes. After her birth, she had hair as bright as a rose, so her parents named her Rose.

Rose has always been a tomboy, so when she was eighteen, she cut off her hair to be rebellious. A year later, it grew out to the top of her ears, and above her neck, curling at the sides. Her mother cried for two days after the cut. She never looked at her daughter the same again.

"But you look like a boy, dear. Young men don't want young ladies who look like boys."

Rose groaned in disgust. "Well, I don't care what boys want, Mother!" She shoved her plate away and stormed away from the table. She ran outside and jumped in her white 1939 Ford Anglia. Her father shook his head, while her mother did her best pretending to be unbothered by her daughter's childish behavior. The only thing other than her music that kept Rose sane when dealing with her parents aggravating ways was driving.

On her way out, Rose picked up her friend Ricky Dupont. He was the same age as Rose, and they were friends since the age of thirteen, Ricky also hailed from a rich family. Although she never fit in with most people around her, he was the closest she had to a real friend. He was a pale, blonde boy with a bubbly personality. While often annoying and immature, he never judged her. He treated her with kindness when no one else would, including her own family. When she went through her rebellious stage, cutting her hair, and dressing like the opposite sex, he still accepted her for who she was.

"Where are we going today?" he asked.

"Anywhere, but here." She said, as she continued to drive.

"We should go fishing! It's a good day for fishing! How about it?" He suggested.

She didn't want to go fishing, but anything was better than going back home. Besides, some fresh air by the lake sounded nice.

"Sure, why not? But, I need to make a stop first. I'm thirsty."

Rose drove to the Negro side of town. The stores in those parts had things Rose's parents never bought. The only person who would come to that side for anything was May, the help. They stopped at one of the local stores.

"We can stop here."

Although skeptic, Ricky agreed as they got out of the car and made their way into the store. Inside, a heavyset, Jewish woman greeted them.

"Hello there! How are you two today? I'm Mrs. Rosenberg!"

Rose smiled, relieved the woman didn't know her. "Nice to meet you, Ma'am! We're just here to get something to drink. Then we'll be on our way."

She hated when people treated her like royalty in public because of her family's social status. After grabbing two drinks from a nearby cooler, Rose gave Mrs. Rosenberg their money at the counter and her and Ricky rushed back to the car. They wanted to get to the lake before nightfall.

Ricky was walking a little too quickly, as he didn't seem to notice a girl in his path. His feet stumbled over hers, causing them to collide, knocking her to the ground.

"Hey!"

Rose heard a loud scream in pain.

"Watch where you're going!" Janet shouted at Ricky.

"You Nigger girls were in my way! Maybe your friend should watch where she's going!"

Rose jumped between the altercation before things got out of hand. As kind as Ricky was, he could be a real hothead, especially when it came to interactions with Blacks.

"Are you okay?" Rose offered the young girl a hand.

"Yeah, I'm okay. Thanks." The young girl took Rose's hand and managed to get back on her feet.

"My pleasure. He's the clumsy one, not you." Rose smiled.

"Darlene! We got to go! Now!"

Janet stood with one hand on her hip, and a look of frustration. Darlene ran toward Janet and they proceeded to walk in the other direction.

"What the hell was that?" Ricky shouted at Rose in anger.

"What? I was just being nice."

As Ricky stared at her, she knew he was mad, but didn't care.

"Relax." She put her hand on his shoulder. They got back into Rose's car and drove away.

They arrived at the lake; Ricky still frustrated from the incident earlier in front of the store.

"Still can't believe those girls! They had some nerve!" Ricky threw rocks into the water to relieve some aggression.

Annoyed, Rose could see where this was going. Ricky's father was the typical southern racist. So, the apple didn't fall far from the tree. While Rose's parents weren't any different, they weren't as cruel either. She threw rocks into the lake with him.

"Well, Ricky, you knocked her down. It wasn't her fault." Rose said, annoyed.

"Are you taking their side? What's wrong with you, Rose? Those people aren't like us."

Rose got angry. She wasn't in the mood for his racist rants. She hated when his father came out of him.

"I'm not taking anyone's side. I'm just saying." "Yeah, whatever..."

Rose walked back toward the car to get the bucket of fish bait. "Can we just fish now? Please? I don't want to argue." She came to the lake to get away from her parents' ignorance, not to deal with his.

During the drive home, Rose couldn't stop thinking about the encounter with the two young girls earlier that evening. To be specific, she couldn't stop thinking about how pretty Darlene was. When Darlene smiled at her, she saw a kind spirit. She also saw a human being, someone who deserved respect. The opposite of what people like Ricky saw.

· · ⚬♋ · ·

THE NEXT MORNING, ROSE awoke to the sounds of yelling coming from downstairs. It was her father. She quickly threw on the clothes that she had worn the day before, that were lying on the floor by her bed, and made her way downstairs to see what was going on.

"You're late! This is unacceptable!" Mr. Caldwell scolded.

He was angry because his chauffeur, Joe, had arrived late and her father had an important meeting to attend.

"I'm so sorry, sir! I promise, sir, it won't happen again, sir!" Joe apologized in hopes that Mr. Caldwell wouldn't fire him.

"You should be thankful men like me are generous enough to give you Negroes work!"

Rose glared at her father after his arrogant statement. She hated when he talked that way. She looked at Joe, and he returned the look. Rose tried not to make eye contact, feeling guilty she couldn't help.

"Thank you, sir, I'm very grateful. It won't happen again." Joe walked out of the house to get the car ready to drive Mr. Caldwell to his meeting.

Walking inside the house through the back door, her mother, Barbra called for her, "Rose, dear, come help me with the gardening."

The last thing Rose wanted to do was be bothered with her mother, but she did love the garden.

"Okay, Mother." An unenthusiastic Rose followed her mother out into the backyard.

Mrs. Caldwell could sense from her daughter's tone that she didn't want to, but she didn't care. The Caldwell family had a huge garden behind their home. She liked to keep herself busy, especially since her husband wasn't emotionally or physically available. He wasn't affectionate or intimate, at least not like he used to be.

"Come pull these weeds, dear." Mrs. Caldwell said.

Rose grabbed the extra pair of gloves her mother kept with her and started pulling the weeds from the plants.

"You and Ricky have been friends for a while, Rose." Her mother began.

"And?" Rose sounded irritated.

"Well, maybe he should take you on a date."

Rose gave her mother a confused look. "A date? Why would he want to do that?"

"Well, you're a pretty girl and you two get along very nicely. I see the way he looks at you."

"He doesn't look at me like that, Mother."

Barbra took a break from watering her flowers. "I think it's time you found you a nice young man, Rose. All the other girls—"

Now angry, Rose interrupted her mother, "I don't care about the other girls, Mother! Why don't you understand that?"

"I don't understand you, dear. You cut off all your beautiful hair. You wear these clothes. What happened to my little girl?"

Rose could see the hurt in her mother's eyes, but it didn't make her words hurt any less. Her mother didn't understand who Rose was, and didn't seem to try.

Rose recoiled her defenses. "I think I need to lay down for a bit." She took off her gloves and went back into the house.

Rose ran up to her bedroom and slammed the door behind her. She reached under her bed for her cigarettes. Jumping on her bed and lighting her cigarette with the nearly empty matchbook, she grabbed one of her records to play something good to ease her mind. "I'm Nobody's Baby" by Judy Garland was playing. She could relate to this song too well. The title described her life to a tee. She was nobody's baby. Not her mother's or her father's, and she hated when they treated her like one. Her parents often pressured her to conform to the lifestyle of her peers. The girls she knew were getting married and starting families. And she was just alone. She had Ricky, but not in a romantic way. She had never had anyone in a romantic way.

She closed her eyes and let Judy Garland's voice flow through her ears. She could get lost in Judy's music for days. Rose liked women and everything about them. She liked how a woman made her feel. But, that was the problem. No one understood how they made her feel. She remembered her mother telling her stories of when she met Rose's father. How she got this passionate, fiery feeling when she first laid eyes on him. That feeling, the same feeling her mother got about her father, was the same feeling Rose got when she thought about women.

Chapter 3

IT WAS A HOT SUNDAY morning. It wasn't summer yet, but spring temps were increasing as it was approaching. On Sundays before church, Darlene and Janet liked to get together to play hopscotch.

"I should go change my dress," Janet said. "This one is new, and mama will kill me if I get it dirty."

"I like that dress on you. It's pretty," Darlene told Janet as she watched her twirl around in her new sky-blue dress.

"Thanks, Darlene!"

"Maybe we should just stop playing and finish getting ready to go," Darlene suggested as the girls headed back into Janet's house to finish preparing for church.

Ms. Benson, Janet's mother, walked out from the kitchen as the girls entered the house. "Did you eat breakfast this morning, Darlene?"

"Yes, Ma'am. I did."

"Okay then. You girls make sure you're ready. We'll be leaving as soon as I finish up in the kitchen."

Like Janet, Ms. Benson was beautiful. She had fair skin. Long hair like Janet's, with green eyes to go with her mixed features. Most of the men in town had a crush on Ms. Benson; even married men stole glances at church, while their wives weren't looking. Darlene was surprised that someone like Ms. Benson was still single.

"Darlene, can you help me tie up my ponytail?" Janet asked, as she handed Darlene one of her blue ribbons that matched her new sky-blue dress.

Darlene stood behind Janet, as Janet pulled up her soft, curly hair. As Darlene tied Janet's hair with the ribbon, she noticed how much more beautiful Janet's skin was up close. Janet literally had not one flaw about her. Inside and out.

"Darlene? What's taking you so long?"

Darlene realized she had spent a little too much time admiring her friend's looks, that the moment became awkward.

"Oh, sorry, I was just making sure it was on tight. That's all." Darlene couldn't help but feel a little embarrassed.

"You girls ready yet?" Ms. Benson asked, walking into her daughter's room.

"Yes, Ma'am," the girls both replied, following behind her as she walked out of the room.

. . ⚮ . .

AS THEY WALKED INTO the church, Pastor Lee greeted them.

"Hello, ladies! Well, don't you look lovely! God blesses! It's a wonderful day to praise the Lord!"

The girls smiled and waved. "Thank you, Pastor Lee!"

Darlene noticed her family sitting in the front row of the church soon after walking in. She proceeded to the front, taking a seat next to her father.

"Hey, baby girl." Her father leaned over and gave her a gentle kiss on the forehead.

"Hey, Daddy."

Nothing made Darlene feel safer and loved than being in her father's presence. The congregation silenced as Pastor Lee read the Scripture.

"But, love your enemies, do good to them, and lend to them without expecting to get anything back. Then your reward will be great, and you will be sons of the Highest! Because He is kind to the ungrateful and wicked. Can I get an Amen?"

Pastor Lee preached in front of his crowd of loyal church members.

With excitement, the congregation shouted back at the pastor, "Amen!"

Darlene sat with her father's arm around her as she listened to the pastor preach about the good Lord. It reminded her of the conversation she had with her grandmother days before.

After church, Darlene ran into Walter Smith. He had caught up with her as her family was heading home.

"Hey, Darlene! I like your church dress today!"

"But, I always wear this dress." She responded flatly.

"I know, but you look extra pretty today! Your hair looks nice, too!"

"Walter, I always wear braids." Her expression didn't budge.

Walter scratched his arm as he was nervous, trying to think of something else to say. Little did he know, unlike Christopher, Darlene picked up on his advances. She knew he had a crush on her, which made her uncomfortable at times, but never too uncomfortable to affect their friendship.

"Hello, young Walter," Darlene's father interrupted, curious of what Walter wanted with his daughter.

"Hello, sir," he replied. "Excuse me, but I was wondering if it was okay if I invited Darlene over to have dinner with my family this evening."

Darlene stopped in her tracks and gave Walter a look of confusion. *Was this his idea of a date?* If so, Darlene wasn't interested at all. She knew she would never forgive herself though, if she declined his offer.

"Dinner? Well, that sounds all right by me," her father agreed.

Darlene was a little bothered that her father hadn't even asked her if she wanted to go.

"But, Daddy, I have to help Grandma with dinner tonight." Darlene had no real plans of assisting her grandmother with dinner that night, but she needed a way to get out of this attempt at a date with Walter.

"Baby, I'll be fine with dinner on my own tonight," her grandmother added, giving Darlene a wink. She thought she was doing Darlene a favor.

"Sounds great!" Walter said with excitement. "I'll be by later to pick you up, Darlene!" He smiled and continued on his way home.

"That's a nice boy, baby girl," her father said, as he put his arm around her, kissing her on her forehead. "He's going to make you a good husband one day!" He laughed.

"Very funny, Daddy," Darlene replied ssarcastically.

Marriage was the last thing on her mind. Especially with Walter. He had always liked him. This wasn't the first time her father had made a joke about Walter pursuing his daughter. It always annoyed Darlene so much. The thought that her father made her feel as if she would have no control over her love life, made her even less interested in having one in the future.

. . ❦ . .

THAT EVENING, AS DARLENE was preparing to have dinner with Walter and his family, she heard a knock on her bedroom door.

"Come in."

"Well, well, well... You and Walter, huh?" Her brother teased as he stood in the middle of the doorway.

Darlene rolled her eyes. "No. Me and Walter nothing. We're just friends. He invited me to dinner to be nice."

"Nice? Boys don't invite girls over for dinner to be nice. He likes you. He wants you to be his girlfriend."

Darlene stopped brushing her hair and shouted, "No way! I'm not gonna be nobody's girl!"

Darren's jaw dropped at his sister's outburst. "Man, sis, I was just teasing. Well, not really, because he really does like you. But, it's okay if you don't like him."

Darlene felt bad for shouting at him. She walked over to him and gave him a hug.

"I love you, Darren."

He smiled and hugged her back. "Love you, too, sis. Enjoy your evening."

"I will."

A knock at the front door interrupted their moment. "Your date is here," Darren joked.

"Darren!" Darlene gave him a slap on the shoulder as he headed back toward his room.

She got one last look in the mirror before heading to the front door. Opening it, she saw Walter standing there, tall and lean with a smile on his face.

"Hello, Darlene, you look very pretty." He complimented with a light smile.

"Thank you."

Her father walked up to Walter and gave him a firm handshake. "You take good care of my little girl now and tell your parents I said hello."

"I will, sir!" He promised.

Darlene gave her father a hug and headed out the house with Walter. She had no idea why her father made it sound like a date when she made it clear it wasn't.

"Thank you for coming." Walter extended his arm out to her.

"Of course." She smiled.

As they reached his house, Walter's mother, Linda Smith, met them at the front door.

"Nice to see you, Darlene! It's been a while. You look lovely!"

"Thank you, Ma'am."

Mrs. Smith was a tall, dark woman, with hair cut short, but she wore it well. Walter's mother was like an African princess, as the bright red lipstick she wore made her smile pop. Everything about her was so graceful.

"Come in, dear, have a seat at the table. Dinner is just about ready." She said with a delicate grin.

They followed his mother inside the house and into the dining room, where his father, Theodore Smith, was impatiently waiting at the table.

"It's about time. My dinner was going to get cold waiting for you two to get here."

Respectfully, Walter pulled out a chair for Darlene to sit. Smiling, she took the seat and sat in silence, not knowing how to reply to Mr. Smith's comment.

"Oh, hush, Theodore," Mrs. Smith scolded. "Pay him no mind, honey. He's just teasing."

Darlene sighed. Mr. Smith was a very intimidating man—tall and dark like Walter—so it was hard to sense when he was joking.

Mrs. Smith brought out the food from the kitchen and placed everything in the middle of the table—fried chicken, candied sweet potatoes, fried squash, and cornbread.

Everything smelled so good. The smell reminded Darlene of her mother's cooking.

"So, Darlene dear, how's school going?" Mrs. Smith asked.

"It's going good." Darlene replied, with her mouth full while chowing down on the golden fried chicken. It was almost better than the fried chicken her grandma made.

"Slow down, girl. You are eating like they don't feed you at home. Look at you, all thin. Like skin and bones." Mr. Smith laughed as he teased her. "I'm just playing with you, girl. How's your father doing? Still working for those rich White folks?"

"He's doing well, sir. He told me to tell you and Mrs. Linda hello." Although Darlene knew Mr. Smith was just teasing, she hated how he spoke about her father.

"Well, that was very sweet of him. Tell him we said hello," Mrs. Smith smiled.

"I'm just saying I can't see how he works for them White folks." Mr. Smith stuffed his face with sweet potatoes. "I'm telling you, girl, stay away from White folks. They don't do nothing, but keep us Black folks down," he rambled on.

"Well, the Rosenberg's are really nice people," Mrs. Smith added.

"Like I said, don't trust the White folks. They aren't about nothing that's helping us."

Walter didn't talk much during dinner. He just enjoyed his mother's cooking and occasionally smiled at Darlene.

"So, what's the deal with you and my son? Y'all going steady now?" Mr. Smith asked Darlene.

She almost choked on her food, a little embarrassed by his question. "No, sir. Me and Walter are just friends."

"Well, either you or that pretty friend of yours, Janet. Now that's a pretty girl, with all that good hair, just like her yellow mama. Probably the only good thing White folks ever do for us Black folks was giving us good hair."

"Theodore, leave the girl alone!" Mrs. Smith interrupted.

"It's getting late. I think Darlene should be heading home now," Walter cut in, with a bit of disappointment in his voice. Darlene knew he had been a little hurt by her saying they were just friends.

Darlene stood up from the table and smiled. "Well, thanks for dinner! It was lovely!"

As she was walking out of the dining room, Mrs. Smith stood up and hugged her. "No problem, honey. Come visit us again soon!"

Walter escorted Darlene out the front door. There were a few minutes of silence as he walked her home.

"Hey, Darlene, can I ask you something?" "Sure, Walter."

"Do you like me?"

Darlene felt a sharp pain in the pit of her stomach. She was starting to get nervous. She knew where this was heading. "Of course, I like you." She answered.

"No, I mean, do you like me...as in a boyfriend?"

The sharp pain roiled around like butterflies in her stomach. She had nothing else to say, but to be honest. "Walter, I like you as a friend, but that's all. I'm sorry."

Walter looked heartbroken. "It's Christopher, isn't it?" Surprised, she couldn't believe he asked that question.

"Christopher? Of course not! I don't like Christopher! Why would you even assume?" Darlene said angrily.

"Well, then who? Why don't you like me? I like you! A lot!"

"I just don't, Walter, and I do not have to explain myself to you! Now leave it at that!"

Darlene was so angry she didn't even want him to finish walking her home. "I'm almost home. You can leave. I'll be fine."

Walter felt guilty for making her upset and realized he was wrong. "I'm sorry, Darlene. I'll see you tomorrow, okay?" He turned around and headed home.

Darlene couldn't explain how she was feeling. Too many emotions floated through her as she could see her house up ahead, lights still on. She didn't even care if she got in trouble for walking home alone. After that, she didn't care about anything.

Chapter 4

"GREAT, IT'S RAINING," Rose mumbled as she slowly climbed out of bed.

It was almost three o'clock in the afternoon and she had to meet Ricky, so they could go fishing. Rose made her way downstairs. Her mother was busy in the dining room having tea with friends. The last thing Rose wanted to do was have any contact with her mother. She tiptoed past the women gossiping in the dining room, making her way to the front door. As she walked outside, she noticed Mr. Jones sitting in his truck, looking frustrated.

"Damn you, car! Damn you! Not now," he mumbled rather loudly to himself.

Rose walked over to the driver's door of his car. "Is everything all right, Mr. Jones?"

"Everything's okay, Miss Rosie. Just out of gas. That's all."

"Well, if you like, I could drive into town and get you some gas."

Shocked by her offer, Mr. Jones protested, "Oh no, I couldn't ask you to do that. I don't mind walking."

"It's no problem, really. I don't mind. You can't walk that far. Especially not around here."

He knew she was right. He gave her a slight smile, thanking her for helping him. "Thank you, Miss Rosie. I appreciate you."

She returned his smile and reached into the back of his truck to get his empty gasoline jugs. "I won't take long. Promise." Rose hurried toward her car, tossing the jugs in the back seat.

Her keeping Ricky waiting was not of importance. She wanted to hurry back before her father noticed Mr. Jones was there and gave him a hard time.

· · ◠◡◠ · ·

DARLENE WAS PATIENTLY waiting for class to dismiss. Walter had been ignoring her all day. He wouldn't even look at her. She knew he was still upset over what had happened the night before. Thankfully, when she got home that night, her father was gone. So, he didn't question her about dinner. When the teacher dismissed the class, Janet caught up with Darlene. Curious about what had happened with Walter. Darlene had left early for school that morning, so Janet didn't get a chance to speak with her all day.

"So... what happened?" Janet asked. "I don't really want to talk about it."

"Oh, come on, I'm your best friend. You got to!"

Darlene let out a loud sigh. "He asked me to be his girlfriend."

"I knew it!" Janet shouted, jumping in excitement.

"Janet! Not so loud!" Darlene said, getting irritated.

"Well, he didn't exactly ask, but he told me he liked me. Then, I told him I didn't feel that way. He got upset and accused me of having feelings for Christopher."

Janet laughed. "I had a feeling he liked you. Well, then what happened?"

"Nothing. I didn't want to talk about it anymore, so he left."

Janet shook her head. "So, are you guys still going to be friends?"

Darlene shrugged. "I don't know. He hasn't spoken to me all day. I hope he forgives me."

Janet leaned over and hugged Darlene. "Oh, he'll get over it. Boys will be boys."

Janet reached her arm over Darlene's shoulder. This was one of those moments Darlene was glad to have Janet as a friend.

They spotted Walter coming toward them. Darlene wasn't in the mood to speak with him.

"Hey, Janet, I'll catch up with you later."

Darlene made her way to the front of the building. She decided to walk around the building, taking a different route home, to avoid having to interact with Walter. It was raining, and she hated taking the longer way home in bad weather, but she just wasn't in the mood to face Walter just yet. A loud car startled her.

"Hey, you! Watch out!" a woman shouted from her vehicle. Darlene had so much on her mind, she didn't see the car that was about to hit her. It was a nice car, different from what she was used to seeing in her town.

"Hey you... girl?" The woman called out to Darlene.

Darlene looked confused.

"Yeah, I'm talking to you." The woman said.

"Do I know you?" Darlene was a little frightened. The woman was White, and Darlene didn't know any White folks other than the Rosenberg family. She knew better than to engage with people she didn't know.

Rose leaned out of the driver's window. "I know you. You're that girl from the store. The clumsy one."

Then, Darlene recognized her, the nice redhead, girl from the incident she had at the Rosenberg's store the other day.

"I almost hit you. You've got to be more careful."

"Sorry," Darlene replied in a soft voice.

"It's fine."

Still feeing awkward, Darlene continued walking away.

"Hey, you need a ride?" Rose asked.

Darlene stopped and turned around. "Who me? No, that's okay. I couldn't."

"Oh, come on, it's raining. I won't hurt you."

Suddenly, Darlene heard a male's voice call out her name. She looked behind her. Janet and Walter were waving in her direction. Rose didn't even have to ask twice before Darlene hurried toward the car and jumped in the passenger's seat. Rose saw Janet and Walter waving at Darlene. She drove off, without even asking Darlene where she lived.

What did I just do? Darlene thought.

She slid down in the seat, trying to avoid someone seeing her.

"So, where do you live?" Rose asked.

"Not too far up that road."

So many feelings were going through Darlene's mind at once. She was riding in a car with a White stranger. Just thinking of the trouble she could be in scared her.

"Why were you in such a hurry to get away from your friends?" Rose asked, interrupting Darlene's inner thoughts.

"I don't really want to talk about it."

"Oh, okay." Rose felt awkward asking.

She looked around Rose's car. It was nice; nothing she was used to seeing. Darlene noticed a fishing bucket in the back seat.

"You like fishing?" Rose asked.

"Me? No."

"I love fishing. I do it all the time. Sometimes with my friend, but usually alone."

Darlene looked at Rose, wondering why she was being so nice to her. She took a moment to study Rose's appearance. Her short hair and boy clothes piqued her curiosity. Despite her unfeminine look, something about Rose was so pretty...

"What's your name anyway?"

"Darlene."

"Well, hello again, Darlene. I'm Rose."

Darlene couldn't stop staring at her. "Your hair, it's so red, like the flower. I've seen red hair before, but not like that. It's so... bright?"

Darlene suddenly noticed they were near the turn that led toward her house. "Oh, turn here."

Rose turned right onto the dirt road. She didn't want her brother or grandmother, or even the neighbors, seeing her getting out of a white woman's car, especially a stranger. She could only imagine the trouble it would cause for her.

"I'm fine here," Darlene said. Rose pulled over and stopped the car.

"Thank you for the ride." Darlene got out of the car, wanting to hurry as fast as she could toward her house before she could be seen getting out of Rose's car. As she was walking away, Rose stopped her.

"Hey, little girl... I mean, Darlene..."

Darlene paused and turned around to see what Rose wanted.

"You should try fishing someday. You'd like it."

Darlene smiled. "I will."

Rose drove away, and Darlene continued her way to the house. When she got home, Grandma Anne was getting dinner started.

"Hey, baby, how was school?"

"It was fine, Grandma."

Darlene noticed her father's shoes weren't by the door. He hadn't returned from work yet. "Where's Daddy?"

"Probably working late. You know how those rich white folks are. He should be home soon. Hopefully, in time for dinner."

"I hope so."

Darlene went to her room to do her homework. She thought about Rose. Other than the Rosenberg family, no other White people had ever been that nice to her before. Secretly, she was hoping they would meet again, even though she knew that was never going to happen.

• • ᴏᶠᴏ • •

BACK ON THE OTHER SIDE of town, Rose rushed back to her home, after getting the gas for Mr. Jones. She felt bad for keeping him waiting. She pulled up and noticed Mr. Jones was impatiently waiting, standing beside his truck.

"Goodness, girl! What took so long?"

"I'm sorry, Mr. Jones. I hurried back as quickly as I could."

"It's okay, Miss Rose. I'm very grateful that you helped me out." He grabbed the jugs of gas and filled up his tank. He threw the jugs into the back of his truck and got ready to drive off.

"Thanks again, Miss Rosie."

"No problem."

She stood by her porch as he drove away. She remembered Ricky. She was honestly in no mood to go fishing anyway. Not to mention it was still raining. She decided to go to her room, enjoy her solitude, and have a smoke like always.

Lighting a cigarette and laying across her bed, she thought about Darlene. Although she could tell Darlene was the shy and bashful type, she still enjoyed being in her company. She thought of how odd it was that she ran into her again. Rose never really believed in coincidences, and she knew they would meet again. At least, she hoped so.

· · ⧄ · ·

THAT NIGHT AT DARLENE'S house, her father had returned just in time for dinner. The family sat down at the table, ready to enjoy Grandma Anne's meal.

"What kept you at work today, Dad?" Darren asked.

"Oh, nothing. I was having some troubles with the truck. That's all. Darlene, baby, I never got a chance to ask how dinner was with Walter's family."

"Oh, it was fine. His parents said hello." She hoped he wouldn't ask anything else regarding dinner at Walter's house.

"I didn't see you after school today with Janet and Walter. Where were you?" Darren asked.

"I took a different way home."

"In the rain?" he questioned.

"Yes, so?" Her brother's little interrogation did not intimidate her. Of course, she couldn't tell them about Rose's ride home.

Her father gave her a look, waiting for her explanation. "Darlene, you know I don't like you walking by yourself."

"I'm sorry, Daddy." Her heart pounded as she tried to figure out a good excuse. "The stupid boys in my class wanted to play another joke on me, so I took a different way, so they wouldn't see me. That's all."

Her father gave her a suspicious look as he bit into his cornbread. "Okay, baby girl. Just don't do it again. You hear me?"

"Okay, Daddy." Darlene smiled; relieved her father didn't punish her or find out about her ride home with Rose.

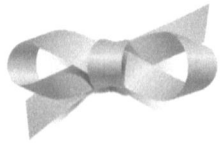

Chapter 5

A WEEK HAD GONE BY, Darlene was in class thinking about her encounter with Rose. All week it had been on her mind, worried that everyone would find out about it. That following day at school, Janet approached her about it, and Darlene concocted a lie about it being one of her father's friends passing by and giving her a ride home. Neither Janet nor Walter got a good enough look at the driver, so she was in the clear, for now. She felt guilty; she hated lying to her best friend.

She and Walter still weren't back on friendly speaking terms. Although he apologized, again, for how he reacted after dinner, Darlene still wasn't impressed. She didn't hate him, though she accepted his apology, she still didn't feel as comfortable around him as she did before. At least now, it was clear and settled that she had no romantic feelings for him.

After class, Walter approached Darlene, smiling, trying his best not to seem desperate. "You look pretty, as always, Darlene. I can walk you home today; carry your books if you want?"

Annoyed by his presence, Darlene wanted him to go away. "Thank you, Walter, but I'm okay." She walked away, trying to avoid any further interaction with him. She cared less about being mean.

That same evening, Rose sat on her porch, smoking a cigarette as she always did. Her father had arrived home, driven by Joe. Rose smashed her cigarette before her father noticed. She ran up to the car to greet them.

"Hello, Mr. Joe! How are you?"

"I'm fine today, Miss Rose, and you?" He tipped his hat.

"I'm fine, sir! Just enjoying the weather today." Rose's father squint-ed, with pursed lips.

"That'll be enough now, Rose." He turned back to Joe. "I expect to see you here first thing tomorrow morning."

"Yes, sir! Seven o'clock! I'll be here, bright and early! Have a good evening, sir!"

Joe got out of the Caldwell's car and walked over to his truck to head home. Rose's father gave her a kiss on the cheek. "How was your day, sweetheart? Occupied with certain habits, again, are we?" Rose reeked of burnt tobacco. He wasn't one to care but knew her mother hated it and didn't want to hear her nagging.

"I've been," she paused, "busy, yes." She gave her father a slight smile.

"Let's get inside, May should have supper on." They made their way into the house.

The Caldwell family took their seats at the table while May served them lamb over a bed of yellow rice and a side of tomato bisque.

"Food looks lovely, May, thank you," Rose complimented as usual.

Her parents, probably frustrated as usual, ignored Rose's comment and resumed eating dinner. Rose knew her extra effort of politeness to-ward May annoyed her parents, which was partly why she did it. To piss them off.

After a few minutes of silence, Mrs. Caldwell finally spoke. "Rose, dear, you remember the Watsons, don't you?"

"Yes, Mom. Why?" Rose was uninterested as she took a spoonful of tomato bisque.

"Well, they're having a function this weekend. You will be attending with your father and I."

Ted and Colette Watson were another rich family that lived in an-other town over. Ted and Rose's father were good friends and, at one point, business partners.

Rose pouted. "What? Ugh! Why do I have to go? I'm not a kid any-more, Mother, you can't make me go to these things anymore!"

Her father interrupted. "You will be going! You will be on your best behavior, and you will be dressing appropriately!"

Rose was seething with Anger.

"Yes, the last thing I need is Colette Watson gossiping about my child with the entire town," her mother added.

Barbara Caldwell and Colette weren't exactly friends but had to associate due to their social statuses and wealthy husbands.

"Why do you care what that hag thinks anyway?" Rose said.

Her mother gasped. "Rose!"

"What?" She shrugged. Not only did she not care for Colette, but her children, Sally and Franklin, weren't exactly the best people to associate with either.

Albert looked at Rose, angry with her behavior. "Rose, don't speak like that to your mother!"

Rose had lost her appetite. "I'm going upstairs." She pushed her plate away and left the table.

"Rose!" her mother called after her.

"Just let her go, dear." Mr. Caldwell said.

They returned to their meals. Rose ran up to her room and slammed the door behind her. It wasn't the function itself that she was mad about, but her parents making her do something she did not want to do. Not only that, her parent's comments about her looks and clothing insinuated that she was an embarrassment to them. To the entire town. The more she thought about it, the more pissed off it made her, so she just decided to turn off her lamp, undress and go to bed.

The next afternoon, Rose was in an irritable mood. She knew she needed to get out of the house but didn't want to be bothered with Ricky. She thought about Darlene, the cute girl with curly hair she met not once but twice. Rose wasn't sure why, but a part of her wanted to see the girl again. That's when she got an idea. It wasn't a smart one, but Rose was always one to take chances. She got dressed, throwing on a pair of denim pants and a white shirt. She made her way downstairs, kissed her mother goodbye and told her she was going for a drive. Rose made her way to the southern part of Durham, to the one place she knew for sure she would run into Darlene again.

Chapter 6

DARLENE WAITED FOR Janet that morning on her porch, for their walk to school together as they did every morning. Janet walked out, books in her hand and a smile, meanwhile Darlene was nervous. She was planning to tell Janet the truth, but fear racked her insides.

"So. I've got to tell you something, but you can't tell nobody, okay?"

Janet's expression grew serious. "What is it?"

"You know that ride home I got that day?

"Yeah?"

"Well, I lied. It wasn't a friend of my daddy's."

Janet stopped, jaw open. "What? Who was it then? A boy—who?"

Feeling she had made a mistake, Darlene decided it wasn't a good time to be honest. "It was a boy. He doesn't go to our school. You don't know him."

"Oh, wow! What's his name?"

"Umm... Ronald. He's sixteen," Darlene lied. "Just don't tell anyone, okay?"

Janet smiled. "Well, okay. To be honest, I had a feeling it wasn't a friend of your daddy's. I mean, that car was too nice. This Ronald must have money. Where did you meet a boy like that?"

Darlene had already felt bad for fabricating the truth and didn't want to finish the conversation.

"Can we talk about something else now? Please? It was just a ride home. Nothing else."

They walked the rest of the way to school in silence, but Janet couldn't help but smile at her friend and her new secret beau.

When school let out that afternoon, Janet couldn't help but bother Darlene about the boy who had given her a ride home.

"You really don't want to tell me more about him? Where is he from? I want to know! Come on!" Janet shook Darlene's shoulder.

"Janet, stop. He's not my boyfriend or anything. So there really isn't more to tell you—" Darlene paused mid- sentence. She couldn't believe her eyes. At least she hoped she was seeing things. There it was, up ahead, the car from that day. Darlene kept walking, hoping it was just her imagination.

Darlene passed by, keeping Janet distracted with nonsense conversation, hoping she wouldn't notice the car. Then, the car drove up next to the girls.

"Hey, you!"

Darlene and Janet stopped.

"Who is that?" Janet asked, squinting her eyes.

Darlene was silent, nervousness rushing through her body. Clenching her schoolbooks, her fingertips began to hurt.

"I know you remember me. Darlene, right? Is that your friend? Hi!" Rose waved at Janet.

Darlene said nothing.

"Wait a minute, this is that car from the other day. Who's that white boy?" Both confusion and concern masked Janet's face.

"That's not a boy," Darlene replied, scared of what was coming next.

"Darlene..." Janet raised her eyebrows, waiting for an explanation.

"Promise not to be mad! Or, tell Daddy, okay? That's Rose. She gave me a ride home that day. And she's not a boy—I lied, I just didn't know what else to say." Darlene blurted out in one breath.

With mouth wide open, Janet didn't know how to respond. "Darlene, what is going on? I don't like this at all."

Rose interrupted them. "Would you like to go fishing with me?" Rose asked Darlene.

"Huh?"

"Would you like to go fishing? With me? Your friend can come, too, if she wants." Rose said.

"I think you should leave us alone." Janet said.

"Janet, please don't tell Daddy, okay?" Darlene asked with pleading eyes.

"What?"

"Just cover for me. One hour and I'll be back, I promise! It's okay. She's my friend. I'll be right back," Darlene tried to convince her.

They looked into each other's eyes, considered each other's feelings, and Janet gave Darlene a nod of approval, even though she didn't want to. Darlene got into the car, and off they drove. Darlene couldn't believe it. She couldn't believe she had just gotten into a car, with a stranger, again. Darlene looked behind her, at Janet still standing there, not sure what to make of any of it. Darlene felt a lump in her throat and her heart pounding through her chest. She wanted to yell for Rose to stop the car, but also wanted her to keep going. She sat there, slumped under to avoid anyone seeing her like the last time she was in Rose's car, with nothing but a blank stare. *This is crazy. What am I doing?* She thought to herself.

"One hour, and I'll bring you back. I promise." Rose caressed Darlene's shoulder as reassurance she could trust her.

Darlene relaxed at her touch. She wasn't sure that everything would be okay by the end of the day, but if she trusted anything, it was that Rose would have her home in an hour.

There were a few minutes of silence before Rose spoke. "I'm sorry."

Darlene looked over at her. "About what?'

"I mean, I shouldn't have approached you like that. You don't even really know me. I didn't mean to scare you or your friend."

It's a little too late for that, Darlene thought. "It's okay." She told her.

"We can turn around if you'd like," Rose proposed.

"No. I'm fine. I think my friend will just say I was at her house if anyone asks. It's just an hour, right? That's not long. My daddy should still be working."

"Your friend seems nice."

"She is. She's the most important person to me, besides my daddy, grandma, and brother, of course."

They finally reached the lake, Rose jumped out of her car to get her things out of the back seat. Darlene got out of the car and took in the beautiful scenery of the lake.

"Come on, this way." With a bucket and two fishing poles, Rose guided Darlene to the spot where she and Ricky usually hung out. They walked down toward the water and took a seat on the edge of the dock. Rose rolled up her sleeves and handed Darlene a pole, with a worm attached to the hook.

"So, what do you usually like to do for fun?" Rose asked.

"I like to cook with my grandma."

"I hate cooking." Rose responded.

"Does your grandma cook, too?" Darlene asked. "My grandma and grandpa died some time ago. My mother doesn't cook. May, the woman who works for us, cooks."

Darlene felt a little awkward, knowing the woman who worked for them was, most likely, a Black woman.

"Oh," Darlene replied, sounding less interested. "Well, what do you like to do?"

"I love music. I want to move to New York City or Hollywood to be a famous songwriter," Rose told her.

"I love New York! That's where my family is from. We moved here after my mother died."

"I'm sorry about your mom. What's it like there?" Rose hoped she didn't sound too insensitive asking about New York after Darlene's comment about her mother's death.

"It's beautiful, fast, and loud. White people are also a little nicer there than here. Not that much nicer, but it's easier to coexist with them in the north I guess."

Rose straightened her posture in defense. "Oh, so I'm not a nice person?"

"Oh, I didn't mean you, of course!"

Rose laughed. "I was kidding."

"Oh." Darlene let out a sigh followed by a slight giggle. For a moment, silence lingered between them before she asked, "Why were you near my school?"

Darlene had been so preoccupied with worrying about whether Janet had spilled the beans, she forgot to ask Rose the most important question.

"I had a fight with my parents. Needed to get away but didn't want to be alone. I needed someone to talk to. My other friend was busy, and I remembered you said you wanted to try fishing, so..."

"You said I should try it, I said okay. That didn't literally mean I wanted you to come to my school."

Rose felt bad and didn't know what to say. There was a small moment of silence between them.

"My daddy would kill me if he found out. I can't believe I came here." Darlene said, growing worried about getting caught.

"Then, why did you? You really didn't have to get in my car." Rose said.

Darlene didn't respond, because she knew Rose was right.

"Pressuring you to come here was stupid, but I'm glad you did it." Rose smiled, trying to ease the tension.

Rose's hand touched her shoulder again. Darlene felt a little embarrassed. Rose was pretty, and she always got nervous around pretty girls.

"I'm glad I came, too." An awkward silence hovered, but they both secretly enjoyed it.

"Besides! I've always wanted to do something bad."

"Janet does bad things sometimes. Her momma doesn't know. Once, she kissed a boy behind the church."

Rose laughed.

"I didn't tell anybody," Darlene continued. "We keep each other's secrets. That's what friends do."

"Well, I hope you don't go kissing boys behind churches, Do you?" Rose asked.

"No! Not me —Ew! I don't like the boys at school or church." Darlene fiddled with the string on her pole.

"I don't blame you. I don't like too many of the guys where I live either."

"Where do you live?"

"On the north side."

"So, you're rich? I know because my daddy works where the rich white people live."

"Yes, my family is well off. But I'm not like them."

"Well, you do dress different. I've never seen a girl wear pants. Not even a poor girl."

"Hey! I like my clothes, thank you very much!" Rose chuckled.

"It does fit you nicely." Darlene complimented.

Rose broke into a wide, open smile. "Really?"

"Yes. Even though girls aren't supposed to wear boy's clothes, you look pretty."

Rose's smile grew bigger.

"I think you're pretty, too. Beautiful. You really are."

Darlene didn't know how to feel about Rose's comment. She liked it but felt wrong for liking it. Something inside her told her it was time to head back home before she got into trouble, if she weren't already.

"I think I should go now." Darlene stood up and brushed off her dress.

"Then home you shall go."

Rose stood up, grabbed the bucket and poles, and they headed back to the car.

• • ⌘ • •

AS THEY NEARED DARLENE'S house, Rose stopped the car at the same spot she had dropped Darlene off before.

"Well, I guess this is goodbye then?"

"I guess so." Darlene got out of the car and looked back at Rose.

"Thank you for coming Darlene." Rose smiled. "How old are you anyway little girl?"

"Thank you for teaching me how to fish, I guess. And I'm fifteen. I'll be sixteen in a few months. So I'm no little girl." Darlene said with her chin raised, holding back a light smile.

"All right then. Goodbye, Darlene."

They waved at each other one last time before Rose drove off.

Darlene walked the rest of the way, alone, smiling. She stopped by Janet's to verify an alibi, if she had one. She would stay there for a bit before heading home. She couldn't wait to tell her best friend about her time at the lake with Rose.

Chapter 7

DARLENE WALKED UP THE squeaky steps of Janet's porch and knocked on the front door. A rush of fear from not knowing whether she was in deep trouble with her father and excitement from being able to tell her best friend about Rose washed over her.

Janet's mother opened the door, greeting Darlene. "Hey, sweetie! How are you?" She stepped aside to invite Darlene into their home. "Janet's in her room. You're welcome to go upstairs." She wiped her hands with a dish towel, as she was preparing dinner when she heard the knock at the door.

"Thank you, Ma'am." Darlene made her way toward Janet's room. She knocked on the door and heard her friend's voice.

"Come in."

Not knowing what to expect, Darlene opened the door and walked in with hesitation. "Hi."

"What is wrong with you, Darlene Jones?" Janet yelled, stomping toward her, grabbing her arm aggressively. "Have you lost your mind?"

"Ouch!" Darlene rubbed her arm, distracted by the pain, not expecting Janet's grip to be so tight.

The girls stood in silence for a few seconds before Janet's anger turned into relief. She flailed her arms over Darlene and gave her a hug so tight she could barely breathe.

"I'm glad you're okay," Janet said in a comforting tone after calming herself.

Darlene wrapped one arm around Janet to hug her back.

Her fingers grazed Janet's long, dark, smooth locks. It was something about the smell and touch of Janet's hair that gave her a strange but satisfying feeling of comfort. They continued to hug.

"So... I guess this means you didn't tell anyone?" Darlene was nervous.

The girls broke their embrace and sat on Janet's bed. "Of course, I didn't. But, I was worried sick! You've got a lot to explain, girl!" Janet buried her eyes deep into her friend's soul, waiting for answers.

Darlene took a deep breath before she told Janet everything—the ride home and Rose was the girl they ran into outside of the Rosenberg's store. She explained how fate and the near-death experience that afternoon, walking home from school had possibly been the start of a new, unsuspecting friendship. However, what she didn't tell her friend was how spending time with Rose gave her a feeling she had never experienced before.

With wide eyes and an open mouth, Janet listened with excitement as Darlene told her everything about this strange White girl. Twirling her long hair, her excitement turned to worry.

"Well, I hope she doesn't come around anymore."

Darlene looked at Janet, a little offended, but knowing she was right.

"You could've gotten in trouble! If your daddy knew—"

"But he won't know!" Darlene jumped up in anger. "Calm down, girl! I won't say anything."

Darlene felt embarrassed by her little outburst. She knew Janet was right about Rose not coming around anymore. Although she had no plans of having another encounter, the thought of never seeing her anymore still hurt Darlene's feelings.

"It was a one-time thing. She won't be coming around here anymore anyway," Darlene explained with false confidence.

Janet saw the disappointment in her friend's eyes. "Besides, if you can keep my secrets about kissing boys at church, I won't tell anyone you went fishing with some strange White girl." Janet nudged Darlene, smiling and teasing.

Janet's mother appeared in the doorway, interrupting the girl's playful moment. "You should be getting home now, Darlene. Janet's got to eat then go to bed."

"Okay, Ma'am. Bye Janet, see you in church tomorrow."

After hugging Janet and her mother goodbye, Darlene made her way out of their home. She walked to her house, clenching her schoolbooks in her arms. She couldn't stop thinking about her time at the lake, happy her best friend had her back. As she entered the front door her grandma was donning a pair of her father's socks.

"Hello, Grandma." Darlene kissed her on the cheek and headed to her room.

What a day.

Chapter 8

ROSE STARED IN THE full-length mirror, lifting the sides of the silk, lavender-colored, ankle-length gown she was wearing. Her mother had gotten it for her to wear to the Watson's party that evening, along with the white heels on her feet. They reminded her of the shoes Judy Garland wore in the Wizard of Oz, which was the only thing she liked about them. She hadn't realized how tall and lanky she looked when her shoulders were exposed. It had been a long time since she had worn a dress, or anything remotely feminine.

"I look ridiculous," she mumbled under her breath.

She heard the door open behind her, and Mrs. Caldwell appeared carrying a pearl necklace.

"Come, dear. We aren't finished just yet."

Standing behind her daughter, holding the necklace, Mrs. Caldwell wore a pink, knee-length dress to show off her slender legs, complimented by soft, red lipstick that made her blue eyes pop. "I haven't been this close to you in so long, I forgot you had those beautiful freckles on the back of your neck." She reached around Rose's shoulders, draping the pearls across her collarbone.

"I look ridiculous, Mother, and my feet ache already from these shoes. I don't like it. This color makes me look like a child."

Mrs. Caldwell snapped the necklace in place. "Oh hush, dear, you look lovely. It would be nice to see you like this more often." She gently caressed her daughter's shoulders. "You look beautiful, dear. I'll tell May to grab my lipstick; it will go well with your dress."

"No! I won't wear lipstick tonight, Mother. That's where I draw the line."

Her mother sighed with disappointment. "All right, fine. But, brush your hair. Well, what's left of it anyway, and be downstairs to meet your father in five minutes."

Rose didn't care about being late to the stupid party, but once again, her mother had made passive aggressive comments about her looks. Rose could've made a snarky remark toward her mother, but she was already in a bad mood, not wanting to go to the party. She decided to ignore her mother, looking over at her brush sitting on the chair of her white waterfall vanity.

Since she had cut her hair, she hadn't used her brush, let alone the vanity. In one last act of rebellion toward her mother, with aggression, she ran her fingers through her three inches of hair, smiling at the reflection of her ruffled hair before making her way downstairs.

"Ah, my beautiful girl, just as gorgeous as your mother." Mr. Caldwell greeted his daughter by the front door, his hand on her shoulder.

"Thank you, Father." Rose smiled.

Mrs. Caldwell, descending the stairs, interrupted their brief father-daughter moment. "Yes, well I did the best I could, dear."

"Well, maybe you'll do better next time," Rose said, sarcastically. "Hopefully, there won't be one, seeing as how I don't plan on going to another one of these dreadful things."

"All right that's enough now, we're going to be late.

Let's make our way to the car." Mr. Caldwell demanded.

Joe was standing by the rear passenger side door, awaiting them. "Why don't you all look nice this evening!" He opened the door for Rose to get in first.

"Thank you, Mr. Joe."

After Albert and Barbara Caldwell settled inside the car, Joe drove them to the Watson's.

Once they pulled up to the Watson's home, Rose felt a knot in her stomach. She had a feeling the evening wouldn't end well. Joe got out of the car and opened the rear passenger door for the family.

Rose held the lower sides of her dress as she walked to the front door with her parents.

"Don't forget to smile, dear," Mrs. Caldwell mumbled to Rose under her breath.

"I won't, Mother." Rose used the same tone while forcing a big smile, attempting to be snarky, as Mr. Caldwell rang the doorbell.

Ted Watson opened the door. "Ah, well, if it isn't the Caldwell's! How are you, my good man? Good to see you and your lovely family this evening!" The two aggressively shook hands, followed by a hug.

"Good to see you as well, friend!" Albert responded with joy.

As they walked inside, Collette Watson greeted them. "Oh, it's great to see you all!" She gave Albert and Barbara Caldwell soft cheek kisses, then her eyes gleamed with excitement as she turned to Rose. "Rose! Little Rose Caldwell! Is that you?" Why, we haven't seen you since you were a wee little thing, it seems!" Collette gave Rose a big hug, squeezing her a little too hard.

Rose felt uncomfortable but played along. "Hello, Mrs. Watson, nice to see you." Rose held a solemn look.

"Al, Barbara, come into the dining room. I want to introduce you to some of our associates you haven't met yet." Ted led them away.

They talked and laughed with other rich men and their wives, going on about mundane things that were of no interest to Rose. After a good ten minutes of listening to all that jabber, she noticed her parents weren't paying attention, so she slipped away, plopping down on a nearby sofa. She felt instant relief of her feet from those shiny white heels, letting out a slight sigh of satisfaction.

"Rose? I knew it was you." Over walked Franklin, the Watson's son.

"Oh, great," Rose mumbled under her breath.

"Who wouldn't notice that red hair of yours, even as short as it is?" Franklin Watson was tall like his father with dirty blonde hair and blue eyes like his mother. "You look beautiful tonight. Word around is you've been running around in rags and boy's clothes; had to see this for myself." A stupid smile covered his face.

Rose was already bothered.

"She actually wore real clothes! Did your maid have to hold you down to get that gown on, Rose?" Sally, Franklin's sister approached her, attempting to join her brother in mocking Rose.

Franklin and Sally laughed, along with a few others, probably friends of theirs.

Angry and humiliated, Rose snapped at Sally, "Oh, go away, jerk!"

Franklin's laughter turned into a smug, angry grin. "Don't talk to my sister like that," he spoke between clenched teeth.

Rose cared less, as Franklin did not intimidate her in the least. "Or what?" Rose stood up, with hands on hips, in a defensive stance. "You're nothing but an annoying creep and a coward."

"Look at you, acting all tough! Just like a man," Franklin said with a smirk. "Are you sure you're not a man? Your breasts are so tiny, barley even there."

Franklin cupped Rose's right breast and, before he could get another word out, Rose punched him hard in the face. He fell backward, nearly knocking over his sister.

"What have you done?" Sally screamed, kneeling to aid her brother.

Rose didn't care about the consequences of her actions. She refused let him assault and humiliate her. Without thinking, she ran for the door, swung it open, and ran down the porch and past Joe, who was waiting by the car, until she couldn't run anymore.

Chapter 9

"BUT, GOD SHOWS HIS love for us, in that while we were still sinners, Christ died for us. Romans 5:8"

Darlene sat on the front pew of church that Sunday morning, with her head resting on Grandma Anne, listening to pastor's words from God.

"Amen!" the congregation shouted in unison.

"Amen," Darlene quietly repeated to herself.

She was in a particularly good mood that morning. The pastor's sermon was on love. How ironic, considering the feelings she had been having, the words from her pastor had touched her in a special way. *Will God still love me if I am different?* Darlene thought. *Why wouldn't He? Grandma always says God loves all His children. Why would someone who doesn't fit man's idea of a perfect human being, be an exception?*

She thought about Rose. How she was so different from most girls Darlene had known.

Can God still love someone like that? If so, then His love for anyone shouldn't be challenged, not even for me.

Her grandmother glanced and noticed that she seemed inattentive. "Baby, are you paying attention? You got your eyes all in the clouds." Grandma nudged Darlene, who still had her head on her shoulder.

"Yes, Ma'am, I am."

Grandma gave her a smile and continued to fan herself. The pastor went on for another hour before wrapping things up. As Darlene got up from the pew, she saw Janet and Walter walking out the church and wanted to catch up with them.

Once outside, Darlene yelled, "Hey, Janet," catching up with her friends.

"Oh, hello, Darlene." Walter greeted her with a less than enthusiastic tone.

Darlene pretended not to notice and turned her attention toward Janet. "Hey, girl! You want to come to my house? Granny is making extra sweet cornbread tonight. Your favorite."

"No, I got to help my momma with the laundry today."

Darlene's smile quickly turned into a frown of disappointment. She wasn't expecting her friend to say no. "Oh."

"I'll see you at school tomorrow?" She was trying to hide the guilt in her voice.

"Yeah. I'll see you tomorrow then."

Janet and Walter continued on their way. Turning around, Janet looked back at Darlene for a quick second. Darlene was wondering what was up with Janet. She seemed to be acting strange. Darlene didn't expect much from Walter, but she did from her best friend. Something wasn't right, and it was making her feel uneasy.

"What's wrong with you, girl?" Joe asked, as he approached his daughter from behind, placing his arm around her right shoulder.

"Nothing, Daddy, I'm okay."

Mr. Jones wasn't convinced. "Well, you don't sound okay, baby."

"Leave the girl alone, Joe." Grandma Anne came to Darlene's defense. She pulled her granddaughter closer toward her. "You know if something is bothering you girl, you can tell me." She hugged Darlene as they walked together.

"Yes, I know, Grandma." Darlene loved her grandma so much; she knew if there was anyone she could confide in, it was Grandma Anne.

• • ⌘ • •

AT THE CALDWELL'S HOME, Rose sat alone in her room.

She was lying on her back, tucked under her covers, still wearing the party gown from the previous night, eyes red from hours of crying. After she ran out of the Watson's party, she ended up walking for twenty minutes before a nice man saw her on the side of the road and offered to take her home. Once she got home, she ran inside, the door slamming behind her. May, who was in the middle of dusting one of the paintings on the wall, was startled by Rose's appearance and called out to her as she bolted up the steps, two at a time, but was ignored. Mr. and Mrs. Caldwell returned home not too long after Rose. They knocked on her door repeatedly, demanding she open it and explain what happened at the party. After a while, the knocking and yelling ceased, and Rose could finally have some peace and quiet, to bask in her sorrow. Franklin's actions at the party were the most humiliating for her...ever. Being an outcast was bad enough, but to put her on display for all to see was beyond hurtful. She got out of bed, undressed and took a bath. After her bath, she didn't bother locking her door. She slipped on her cream-colored nightgown and crawled back into bed. She was ready to deal with her parents and the consequences to follow.

The next morning, as she lay lazily in bed, she heard footsteps approaching her room, and in walked her mother. She stood by the doorway for a few seconds, looking at her daughter, as if she were trying to figure out who was this stranger sitting before her. Mrs. Caldwell leaned against the doorjamb with crossed arms.

"Rose Elizabeth Caldwell, you better explain yourself this instant!"

Rose gave her mother an emotionless stare and sat on the edge of her bed, with no response.

"Well? Your father and I are very angry with you and your behavior last night at the Watson's. You hit Franklin? What would make you to do such a thing?" Mrs. Caldwell questioned, with dismay in her voice. "I told you not to embarrass us! But did you listen? No, instead you go around hitting people, a boy at that, like some foolish little girl!"

Rose's blood was boiling, listening to her own mother make her out to be the enemy. She heard her father coming toward her room. He appeared and stood next to his wife.

"Well, what is the meaning of all this? Your behavior last night was unacceptable!" Mr. Caldwell, although angry with Rose, didn't sound as harsh as his wife did when speaking to his daughter.

Rose felt cornered, but there was no way she was going to tell them what really happened at the party. She took a deep breath and spoke. "He called me ugly." It wasn't the truth, but she knew it was better than telling them what really happened.

Mrs. Caldwell dropped her arms at her sides. "What?"

Mr. Caldwell's anger quickly turned into laughter. "My daughter, tough as rocks, just like your old man."

Rose looked at her father with a slight smile.

"Ted and I have been good acquaintances for some time now, but I've never cared for that boy of his."

Rose giggled. She was relieved that her father didn't scold her to death like her mother wanted to.

Gasping, Mrs. Caldwell looked at her husband, with her mouth wide open at his response. "Albert! Franklin is the Watson's son. Rose cannot go around hitting people over a... a childish remark!" She was even more furious now.

"Calm down, dear, Rose knows she was wrong and I'm sure it won't happen again." "Yeah, because I'll never show my face around those people again," Rose barked.

"You insufferable, little brat!" Mrs. Caldwell yelled. "All right, that's enough now. I think the girl has learned her lesson now, Barbara, let's leave her be."

Albert gestured for his wife to leave the room with him. Of course, she was still furious, but decided to put on her calm face as they left the room, and let the situation die...for now.

As her parents left the room, Rose let out a sigh of relief. After everything that happened the night before, the last thing she wanted to deal with was her parents.

A few moments later, a car horn blared from outside. She jumped up and walked toward her window, knowing it could only be one person, and she was right.

"Ricky!" Rose yelled, happy to see her friend.

Still in her nightgown, she ran out of her room and down the stairs to the front door. As soon as she opened it, Ricky was getting out of his car and walking toward her. She ran to him and flung her arms around him in excitement. He was surprised to see this type of reaction from her.

"Rose, pal, I see you're happy to see me," Ricky joked. He unclenched her arms from around him. "A little too happy."

Rose realized what she had done, and embarrassment flushed her cheeks, turning as red as a tomato. She punched Ricky in the shoulder, reestablishing her dominance.

"Whatever! You know it's not like that. Just haven't hung out in a while, that's all."

"Yeah, yeah." Ricky rubbed his shoulder. He looked her up and down. "Go get dressed or something, will ya?"

Rose looked down at her nightgown. "Let's go to my room, I don't really want to go out today."

"All right."

They walked inside and made their way to Rose's room. May walked by, giving Rose and Ricky a good-morning nod. Rose, of course, returned the greeting. But Ricky being his usual self, ignored May and continued to follow Rose to her room. They sat down on her bed. Rose dug between her mattresses and grabbed her pack of smokes and matches. She took one out of the box and shoved it in her mouth, lighting it with the matchstick.

"So, I heard about what happened at the Watson's party. You really gave Franklin a shiny new one, huh?"

For a second, she was annoyed that he had heard about it so quickly, and then remembered that it was a party full of rich folks, who mostly knew each other, so she wasn't surprised.

"Yeah." Rose puffed on her cigarette.

"Well, what did he do to deserve that?" Ricky was desperate to hear her side of the story.

Rose wanted to tell him so badly, but not badly enough to risk going through the embarrassment of talking about it and having to relive that situation.

"He called me ugly, so I socked him."

Ricky laughed. "Man, you really are the toughest person I know! That's why you're my favorite girl! Anyone would be a fool to mess with you."

Rose watched him as she finished her cigarette. She wondered if he would stick around if he knew the real her. If anyone would.

Chapter 10

STANDING NEXT TO GRANDMA Anne in the kitchen, Darlene shucked the husks of corn, helping her prepare for dinner.

Grandma was singing *Strange Fruit* by Billie Holiday, as Darlene was humming along in sync. She loved to listen to her grandma sing, but didn't enjoy singing herself, adding it to her list of things she wished she were good at doing. It had been a week since her odd encounter with Janet at church, and when she saw her in school, her behavior still seemed to linger. Even when Darlene wanted to play hopscotch after school, something they did often, Janet declined.

Hopscotch was their favorite thing to do together, which made Darlene feel like she was losing her only friend. The pain from those thoughts distracted her from Grandma's singing, and she stopped humming along.

"Darlene Jones, if you don't turn that frown upside down, little girl." Grandma Anne yanked Darlene's right earlobe, which she did whenever she got frustrated with her grandchildren.

Darren walked into the kitchen, planting a big smooch on his grandma's cheek. "Darlene's sad because Janet's not her best friend anymore." Darren enjoyed teasing his sister.

"Is this true, baby?"

Darlene was still looking down at the husks, shucking away. The last thing she wanted to talk about was the issue with Janet. "I don't know if she's mad at me, but she acts like it."

"Well, why would she act like that?"

"Because Darlene's so ugly she can't stand to look at her anymore." Darren laughed at his joke, sticking a finger into the chocolate frosting his grandmother had sitting on the table for the cake she was baking.

"Oh, hush boy! Whatever it is, I'm sure she'll get over it and you two will be back as best friends in no time."

Darlene didn't say anything, but she appreciated her grandma's optimism. Although Janet hadn't admitted it, she was sure Janet's strange behavior toward her was because of Rose.

They heard a car pull up to the house, knowing it was Joe coming home from work. The front door opened, and they could hear Joe talking to someone, as he walked inside.

"Looks like we have a visitor." Grandma Anne said.

A visitor? Who? Darlene thought. Besides Janet, no one really came to the house to visit.

"Mama Anne! Darlene and Darren! Come in here and say hello to our dinner guest!" Joe yelled from the front room of the house.

Anne grabbed two dish towels, handing one to Darlene to wipe their hands. They walked out to greet the stranger and as soon as Darlene laid eyes on their guest, she froze. Her stomach was hurting, as if someone were grabbing her intestines and squishing them up like grapes. Her heart pounding, she was overwhelmed. Standing next to her father was Rose.

"This is Rose, everybody. She's the daughter of the man I work for." Joe introduced.

"Hello, nice to meet you all!" Rose shook Darren's hand and gave Grandma Anne a hug.

She saw Darlene standing there and could tell she was just as shocked. Equally nervous and surprised, Rose didn't look so obvious. She extended her hand toward Darlene, gesturing for a handshake. A hug wasn't appropriate, so she remained a stranger.

"Hi, you must be Darlene. I've heard a lot about you. You're a beautiful girl, just like your father said." Rose said.

"Thank you." Darlene shook Rose's hand with hesitation but played along.

Oh my, God! Oh my, God! This can't be happening. This can't be real. That can't be her.

Darlene didn't know what to think. A million thoughts were going through her head at once.

"Don't be scared girl, Rose won't bite you," Joe said. "She's a little nervous, ain't used to being around White folks."

"What brings you here tonight, Miss Rose?" Grandma Anne was being polite, but quite curious.

"Mr. Joe was having car troubles, so I gave him a lift home and he invited me to stay for dinner."

"Well, then, it's nice to have you! Darren, grab a seat for Miss Rose!"

Darren walked to the other side of the sitting room to grab a chair for Rose. Darlene stood frozen in place, wearing a blank expression. Rose glanced at her, smiling, but trying to avoid prolonged eye contact. The last thing she wanted to do was make Darlene feel any more awkward then she already did. Darren sat the chair near the unlit fireplace.

"Here you go."

"Thank you." Rose sat down in the hard, sturdy wooden chair. It was a bit uncomfortable, but she didn't want to be impolite.

Grandma Anne returned the kitchen to finish cooking, with Darlene hurrying behind her.

"Darlene, baby, come here," Mr. Jones called out to her.

Darlene walked a slow gait into the sitting room.

"Both of you aren't too far from each other in age. Rose is nineteen."

Ha, yeah, I know.

Darlene gave a little smile, acknowledging her father's comment.

"Why don't you two get to know each other a little? Keep Rose company while your grandma finishes up with dinner." Mr. Jones suggestion felt more like a demand, seeing as how Darlene really had no choice.

"Okay, Daddy."

"How about we go outside? Your father tells me you like to play hopscotch? That sounds fun. I've never played that game before." Rose suggested.

"That sounds good. Go ahead, baby girl." Joe agreed.

Rose got up from her chair and walked toward the door, with Darlene turning to walk to her room to get her chalk, then following behind. The girls made their way outside. Before Rose could get a word in, Darlene's nervousness had switched to anger.

"My father works for you? You know my father! He knows you!" Darlene said in a loud whisper. She didn't want her family hearing any of this conversation.

"Calm down. I'm just as surprised as you are. My heart nearly fell out of my ass when I walked into your house and saw you."

"Does he know? Wait, that's stupid. Of course, he doesn't. I'd be dead." Darlene said.

"Why would I tell him anything?"

Darlene stood on the porch, with her arms crossed, glaring at Rose. After taking a deep breath, she sat in one of her grandmother's rocking chairs. Rose followed and sat in the other rocking chair, the one Darlene normally sat in when she spent quality time with her grandmother.

"I can't believe my father works for you." Darlene said.

"He doesn't. He works for my father."

"Same thing." Darlene responded snidely, as if that was supposed to make a difference.

This is a disaster. Darlene thought. Clearly, this had to be a sign from God that Darlene had no business getting involved with Rose in the first place. Feeling guilty, Rose realized this entire situation would cause more consequences for Darlene than her.

"I'm sorry for putting you through all of this. I can leave, if you want me to. I shouldn't be here anyway." Rose got up from the chair. "I'll go inside and tell your father something came up."

"No!" Darlene grabbed Rose's arm, preventing her from walking back inside. "I want you to stay."

Realizing what she said came off more intimate than she wanted it to, Darlene caught herself and tried to switch her tone. "I mean, I would like for you to stay. It would be impolite if you left."

Rose moved back toward the chair and resumed her seat. She wouldn't admit it, but she didn't want to leave and was glad Darlene suggested otherwise. Darlene was quiet, fiddling with strands of her hair. Looking at the raggedy dress she wore, she was suddenly overwhelmed with embarrassment. That nervous feeling crept up her spine again.

Rose sensed the awkwardness between them. "Your family is really nice. Given the circumstances, it really is nice to see you again, Darlene. I had a really good time with you at the lake and I was hoping we would meet again."

Darlene smiled. "Yes, me, too." She was flattered and didn't care if it showed. Now that the awkward stage of fear and guilt had subsided, Darlene leaned back comfortably, rocking the rocker, with both hands on the arms. Smiling, she looked up at the sky.

"So, what's it like where you live?" Darlene asked.

"It's nothing special." Rose tried to water down her privileged lifestyle.

"I mean, like how big is your house and stuff? I bet it's nice. I bet the sun shines into your big ol' windows every morning!" Darlene couldn't help but imagine how nice it must be.

"We've got a garden."

Darlene's eyes widened with excitement. "A garden! I love flowers!"

"Oh, do you now? What's your favorite?" Out of all the things Rose ever did with her mother growing up, helping her in the garden was her favorite. Now, being older, she didn't spend much time with her mother, but when she did, it was in the garden.

"My favorite flowers are daisies. I also like roses—" Darlene paused, realizing what had just come out of her mouth.

Roses? Rose? That was stupid! Why did I say that?

Darlene was embarrassed, looking over at Rose, who was also looking back at her but looked away, smiling. Darlene knew she had caught on to what had just happened. They both were silent, trying to recover from that awkward moment.

"I thought we were supposed to be playing hopscotch?" Rose tried to change the subject. She stood up from the chair and jumped down off the porch. "Well? Get out that chalk. Show me how to hopscotch!"

Smiling, Darlene stood and grabbed the chalk from her dress pocket. She walked down off the porch toward Rose and knelt, drawing ten squares and ten numbers. She stood on one foot in the first square, tossed a small rock she had picked up off the ground toward the last square, and hopped down to the tenth number.

"It's easy. See? Now your turn."

Rose followed Darlene's steps, tossing the rock and copying her one-foot, two-foot pattern. Their game went on for a few more minutes before Rose got to the tenth square one last time.

"Well, that was fun, wasn't it?" Rose sounded a bit winded.

"Yeah it was." Darlene thought of Janet. Her smile slowly turned into a frown, thinking about the situation with her friend being upset with her. Or, so she assumed.

"What's got you down, girl? Rose walked closer to Darlene.

Darlene didn't like talking about the situation but felt she could open up to Rose. "My friend, she won't talk to me and I don't know why. Well, I do, kind of. I think it's because of you. I told her the truth about the ride home you gave me, the lake, everything. At first, I thought everything would be fine with us, but I guess I was wrong."

Rose saw the pain all over Darlene's face.

"She's been avoiding me since church last Sunday."

Darlene walked over to sit on the porch steps. Rose followed behind, sitting down next to her. She put her arm around Darlene.

"If she wants to end your friendship for whatever reason, that's her loss."

Darlene looked up at Rose. As sad as she was about Janet, Rose made her feel a little better, even if it was temporary.

Darren opened the door, not expecting to see the girls in that position, with Rose's arm still around Darlene. "Daddy said dinner is ready," he said in a timid voice. He didn't look too thrilled to see them looking so intimate. The girls got up and made their way inside the house.

Dinner consisted of chicken, corn, mustard greens, and cornbread. At the table, Rose sat next to Mr. Jones. She wanted to sit next to Darlene but didn't want to bring unnecessary attention to them. Darlene didn't seem to mind, as she sat next to her grandma.

"Food looks delicious, Ma'am. Thank you." "You can call me Ms. Anne, honey."

Rose smiled at Grandma Anne, taking a big bite out of the cornbread. The rest of dinner consisted of Grandma Anne telling funny stories from Mr. Jones' childhood. They laughed and enjoyed her storytelling, with Darlene sneaking glances at Rose between bites of her corn. At one point, Rose caught her looking and she nearly choked. What Darlene didn't see was Darren, who had noticed her looking at Rose. He was already suspicious after seeing them outside, so close.

. . ⚬∿⚬ . .

AFTER DINNER, ROSE helped Grandma Anne clean up after everyone, while Darlene and Darren got ready for bed. As Darlene was in her room, brushing her thick coils, already set to end the night in her sleeping gown, Rose entered.

"I wanted to get a proper goodbye."

Darlene, surprised by Rose's visit to her bedroom, held a blank stare, her brush still in her hand.

Rose walked over to Darlene and gave her a hug. "Bye, Darlene Jones. It was a pleasure having dinner tonight."

Rose let go and proceeded to walk out.

"Wait." Darlene walked over to her bedside, grabbed her little flowerpot, with the daisy in full bloom, and walked over to Rose.

Darlene extended the flowerpot to Rose. "I want you to have this."

Smiling, Rose accepted Darlene's gift. "Your favorite flower," Rose remembered.

Darlene's dark brown eyes locked on Rose's grey eyes.

Neither could prepare themselves for what happened next. Warm like a bright summer day, there was a silence like the world had ended; only Darlene and Rose left standing. That's what Darlene's first kiss felt like. Things that never made sense before were now as clear as they had ever been.

Chapter 11

THREE DAYS. THAT'S how much time had passed since Rose had dinner with the Jones's, and Darlene found out that her father worked for the parents of Rose Caldwell, the strange but cool, pretty, and sweet girl who she had formed a random friendship with from a ride home. It had been two days and 10 hours to be exact, since the kiss.

That night after the two had shared an unbelievable and sinful moment, Rose who, was mortified by what had taken place, left without even saying another word to anyone.

Darlene rushed to close her bedroom door, with her hands clasped over her mouth. She jumped into bed, pulling the covers under her neck, and staring at the wall. She couldn't sleep. After trying to process what had just happened, she didn't think it was possible to sleep again, ever. The next morning Grandma Anne and Darren tried to get her up for school, but she told them she wasn't feeling too well. She pulled the same stunt the next day, avoiding school for the second day in a row.

On the third day, Darlene knew she couldn't fake her sickness any longer. Besides, Grandma Anne had been boiling ginger root in hot water and having her drink it, a home remedy for tummy aches. It was nasty and even worse because there was no real tummy ache. Just a gut full of shame.

Darlene got out of bed and performed her usual morning routine to get ready for school. She hadn't thought about anything but the kiss since the moment it happened. Janet had even come by the house yesterday, worried since Darlene hadn't been to school. Darlene declined her visit. Although it would've been a good idea to spend some time with Janet, it just wasn't a good time. Darlene had too much on her mind and their friendship would have to wait.

"Oh, you're feeling better today, baby?" Grandma Anne entered Darlene's room. She must've heard her up and moving around.

"Yes, Grandma."

"Good, you've missed enough school." Grandma Anne smiled and hugged her.

After Darlene was dressed and ready, she met Darren outside to walk to school. She wasn't worried about running into her father, as he left every morning before they rose. As she walked onto the porch, Darren was standing there, giving her a strange look. Ignoring him, with her books held close to her chest, walked ahead. Whatever he was up to, she wasn't in the mood.

"Look who decided to feel better suddenly. Some tummy ache that must've been."

Darlene turned around, looking at her brother with a smug look on his face. "Yeah, so?"

"I think you were faking it."

"Shut up, stupid." Darlene kept walking, further away from him.

Darren jogged to catch up. "What's wrong with you?" "Nothing, I had a tummy ache, Grandma's ginger water worked and now I feel better. Now leave me alone."

Darren could tell she was serious, so he stopped teasing her. They walked the rest of the way in silence.

When they arrived at school, Darlene became nervous. It had been a few days since she had talked to Janet or Walter, not that she cared that much for Walter anyway. She didn't know what to expect. Would Janet finally explain herself?

She walked into her classroom and Janet, who was sitting in her usual seat, got up and ran to hug Darlene. It felt nice; she really missed her best friend.

"I came to see you while you were sick, but your grandma said you didn't want any visitors. I've missed you at school."

Darlene smiled. "I missed you, too." She then noticed that Walter and Emily were sitting in their seats, staring at her. Emily whispered in the ear of one of her friends. They both giggled.

Ms. Fontaine then called for everyone to take their seats, so she could begin her lessons. Darlene took her regular seat by the window, so she could gaze out and daydream. She had a lot to daydream about today. She had been thinking of Rose all morning.

I can't believe I kissed a girl! What if Daddy finds out? Will Rose tell? No, she wouldn't. We're friends, right? Besides, she would get in trouble, too. I mean, kissing girls is wrong. Darlene's mind filled with the worst thoughts. Her stomach began to hurt. *She probably hates me now. Rose hates me. God hates me. Oh, no.*

Sitting on the right of Darlene, Janet noticed she was distracted. "Hey." She poked Darlene with a pencil. "What's going on in that head of yours?"

"Huh? Oh, nothing." It would be a cold day in hell before she told Janet about what happened between her and Rose.

"All right then." Janet wasn't convinced, but Darlene's daydreaming wasn't exactly an uncommon thing for her to do, so Janet shrugged it off and focused her attention back to Ms. Fontaine.

After school, Janet and Darlene were exiting the building when Emily stopped them. She bumped the girls on purpose and wedged between them from behind, stopping them in their tracks.

"I heard you've got a boyfriend. Is this true, Darlene Jones?" Emily flipped her long, light brown hair over her left shoulder.

"A what? No."

"Well, that's what Janet says. That you've gotten yourself a boyfriend. Well, who is it?" Emily demanded. "It's that White boy from the store, isn't it?"

"What? Janet what is she talking about?"

"I didn't tell her Christopher was your boyfriend. I swear!" Janet said.

"So, he is!" Emily's eyes grew wide.

"No! I don't have a boyfriend! If I did, it definitely wouldn't be Christopher!" Darlene was furious. She had no idea where these allegations of some mystery boy were coming from. Then she remembered that Janet knew about Rose. But, a boyfriend? What exactly did she tell Emily? Darlene wondered.

"Well, you heard wrong, because there is no boyfriend." Darlene told Emily.

"I should've known. A boy would have to be blind to like you. I don't even see why Walter likes you." A smug grin appeared on Emily's face.

Darlene was hurt. Emily saying something so mean didn't surprise her because that's who she was, a mean, callous girl. Without responding, Darlene ran away from them.

Janet ran after Darlene. "Wait!" She caught up with her. "I never told her you were dating Christopher. She made that up herself."

"Well, what did you tell her?" Darlene groaned.

"She asked why you and I hadn't been together lately, and I just told her that you had been spending time with someone else. That's all. I swear to God."

"Well, why does she think I have a boyfriend? Or that it's Christopher? Why does everyone think I like him? Ugh!" Darlene grew more frustrated.

"She assumed it was a boy. She asked if it was Walter, I said no. The rest was all her."

"So, is this why you've been acting odd and avoiding me? Rose? I knew it." Darlene's suspicions had been correct. "It was one time. You're my best friend, you know that."

"I know, but you going to the lake with her was a bad idea. I still don't feel too good about it, and I was pretty upset about you lying about her at first. I could tell you really like her. I just don't want you doing anything stupid. Like seeing her again."

Darlene remembered dinner. She wanted to tell Janet, but knew it wasn't a good idea. At least, not yet.

"Look, don't worry about Emily; you know how mean she is." Janet told her. "Don't worry about Walter either; he's just mad because you broke his little heart."

Both girls laughed. It felt good to have her friend back and things felt normal again. But, Darlene knew things were anything but normal. She kissed a girl and it was eating her up inside. She couldn't tell anyone, and she didn't even know if she would even see Rose again, which hurt even more.

When Darlene had arrived home, Darren was already there. He was sitting on the porch, tossing rocks, while Grandma Anne sat in her rocking chair, donning one of her Joe's socks. With Emily holding her up about that boyfriend nonsense, he had at least a ten-minute head start. She walked up, sliding past her brother, giving Grandma the usual hello kiss on the cheek. As she walked inside the house, heading straight to her room, Darren followed.

She threw her books on the bed and sat down. "What do you want?"

Darren stood by the door, leaning against the doorframe with his arms crossed. "Something is different about you, and I'm going to figure it out."

"Figure what out?"

"Why Janet was acting so strange toward you, and that girl Daddy had over for dinner. You two looked like you were the best of friends. You had never even met her until that night. Don't get me started on that tummy ache."

Darlene couldn't believe him. He had some nerve meddling in her business. Mentioning Rose? She didn't even think he paid them any mind. The last thing she needed was her brother getting involved with anything having to do with her and Rose.

"Janet was upset because someone at school told her that I liked Walter. Turns out she likes him, so I guess she was jealous or something. But that's over and we're friends again."

"Uh huh." Darren didn't sound too convinced. "And Rose was just being really nice to me. Besides Janet, I don't have any friends, so I enjoyed her company. Also, my tummy ache was real! I told you that already. Now go on and leave me alone, before I tell Daddy when he gets home."

Although Darren may not have been completely convinced, he went on his way to do homework. Whether he believed Darlene or not didn't matter to her, she felt like her excuses were good enough. Maybe not good enough to keep her brother off her back for good, but good enough for him to leave her alone for a while. Darlene slammed her face into her pillow, wanting to forget this disaster of a day.

Chapter 12

TWO MONTHS HAD GONE by since Darlene had seen Rose at dinner that night. It was a Tuesday afternoon, school was out for the summer, and it was Darlene's sixteenth birthday. Mr. Jones had just gotten home from work. He kicked off his shoes and took off his hat, as he made his way inside. Grandma Anne was in the kitchen finishing up the birthday dinner she had been preparing.

"Darlene, baby, come here. I've got a gift for you."

Darlene was in her room, trying to detangle the knots in her hair so she could wear her hair down for her birthday without any troubles. She was wearing a pink dress, with a navy-blue plaid design, with black shoes she normally wore to church. She ran out to greet her father. He leaned over so she could give him a hug and a kiss.

"Happy birthday, baby girl! You're growing up so fast!"

Darlene saw the flat, square box in his hand, wrapped in brown paper with a yellow ribbon. Her eyes popped with excitement. "For me? What is it?" She jumped up and down holding her father's arms, waiting for him to hand her the box.

"It's a gift. From Rose. You remember her, from dinner."

Darlene stopped jumping. The last thing she was expecting was to hear from Rose again, let alone get anything from her.

"How did she know my birthday was today?"

"I mentioned it a few weeks ago. I guess she remembered. I'm tired, let me relax a little before dinner is ready, then we can celebrate my baby's big day." Mr. Jones gave his daughter a kiss on the cheek and walked to his room.

Darlene ran to her room, anxious to open the box. She couldn't tell if she was excited to see her gift, or that it showed Rose cared enough to think about her. She jumped on her bed, untied the yellow ribbon, and tossed it aside. She ripped at the brown paper. It revealed a white, cardboard box. As she opened it, she gasped at the beautiful oval, sapphire and diamond pendant. The sapphire was deep blue, almost like the sky at night, surrounded by diamonds, like the sun—a blue, oval diamond sun. She was so distracted by the beautiful necklace, she didn't notice a folded piece of paper had fallen out of the box, landing next to her, on the bed. She unfolded it. It was a letter from Rose.

Dear Darlene,

First, I want to apologize for my sudden departure from your home that night. It was rude, and I am terribly sorry. I'm sure you have been having a hard time after the kiss, and I feel I must apologize for that as well. Not because I didn't want it to happen, but because I crossed the line. Also, there is something I want to tell you, but a letter won't do this any justice. Do you remember the first moment we met? At that store where I bumped into you? I would like to see you again, Darlene. Assuming you are reading this on Tuesday, I will be there the following Saturday, at noon, waiting for you, if you decide to come. I hope you will, but I understand if you do not. If you decide not to, I won't be bothering you any longer. But you must know that I think you are the sweetest and most beautiful girl I have ever met. You may have been confused that night after we kissed, but I wasn't.

P.S., I hope you like the gift. My parents gave it to me on my sixteenth birthday. Now it's yours. Happy Birthday.

With Love, Rose C.

The next ten minutes, Darlene sat there with a blank stare, holding the paper in her hands. She had absolutely no words. Rose had given her this beautiful necklace, which probably cost a fortune. Then this letter. She kept reading the last two sentences over and over.

But you must know that I think you are the sweetest and most beautiful girl I have ever met. You may have been confused that night after we kissed, but I wasn't.

She was trying to figure out what all of this meant. Then the part about wanting to meet again. She was referring to the Rosenberg's store. Darlene couldn't possibly do that. The first two times were risky enough; Rose was mad to recommend something so dangerous. Anyone could see them together, and it would get back to her family this time, for sure. She heard someone coming toward her room, so she stuffed the paper under her blanket.

"Darlene, baby, dinner is ready. Is that the gift from your little friend?" Grandma Anne stood in the doorway and pointed at the white box.

"Yes, it is. It's a necklace, look." Darlene walked over to her grandmother, showing her the jewelry, still in its box.

"Oh, my Lord! That's beautiful!" Grandma Anne clasped her hand over her mouth, as she gazed over the magnificent necklace. "She gave that to you? Why would she give you such an expensive thing?"

"Well, she's rich. Rich White folks are always giving people nice things, I guess."

Darren came to see what all the fuss was about. "Whoa, what is that?" he exclaimed, looking just as shocked as their grandmother.

"It's a necklace, stupid."

"Oh, hush girl!" Grandma Anne snapped. "Darren, that young lady Rose gave this to your sister for her birthday. Isn't it wonderful?"

Darren didn't look too pleased. He was already weary of his sister's behavior. He let it go after the last time he confronted her, but this necklace had him wondering again about this Rose girl's relationship with Darlene.

"I'm hungry, can we eat now?" Darren whined, trying to end Darlene's moment.

"Well, I suppose we don't want the food getting cold. Come on, let's show your father your gift."

Grandma Anne escorted them both to the kitchen where Mr. Jones was already sitting and waiting. As they approached the table, Darlene pulled out a seat next to her father, placing the white box on her lap. Darren sat next to Grandma Anne.

Since it was Darlene's birthday, she got to have whatever she wanted for dinner. It was a family tradition that whenever it was someone's birthday, they got to pick the meal for the family that evening. Of course, Darlene chose Grandma Anne's special pancakes, with fried chicken, cornbread and mashed potatoes. They said the usual dinner prayer, led by Mr. Jones, and then dug in.

"Darlene, baby, what was in the box Rose gave you?" Her father asked.

Distracted by Grandma Anne's delicious meal, she almost forgot to show him. She pulled it up from her lap and opened the box.

"Good God Almighty! She gave that to you?" Mr. Jones' eyes widened, like he had never seen anything like it. Well, he hadn't. Black folks didn't walk around wearing jewelry worth hundreds of dollars. He picked up the necklace and dangled in in front of him.

"It's beautiful, baby girl. Rose really is something special. I'll be sure to thank her for you. I almost forgot, since we are showing gifts, I guess I can give you yours now." He placed the necklace back in its box and reached into his pocket, taking out a pocket watch. "I bought it from a farmer down on Oak Road. Thought you might like it."

"Thank you, Daddy, I love it!" Darlene planted a big kiss on his cheek and put the watch into one of her dress pockets.

She felt guilty about the gift from Rose. It seemed inappropriate, considering Darlene's family didn't have a lot of money. It was like a slap in the face to her father, who worked so hard every day, only to be financially emasculated in front of his family on his daughter's birthday.

But Mr. Jones, being the type of man he was, didn't seem bothered by it.

"Well, you got some pretty lovely gifts today, baby."

"Thank you, Grandma." Darlene looked around the table at her family and thought how grateful she was to have such wonderful people in her life.

That night, after dinner, Darlene was lying in bed, snuggled under her covers with the letter from Rose in one hand and the necklace around her neck, twirling the sapphire stone between her fingers.

I would like to see you again, Darlene. Assuming you are reading this on Tuesday, I will be there the following Saturday, at noon, waiting for you, if you decide to come.

She must've read that letter at least a two dozen times. Specifically, the part about Rose wanting to meet again. As wild as it sounded, Darlene wanted to go. She knew it was a bad idea, but that didn't change that in her heart and mind she knew she needed to see Rose again. She was also curious about what it was that Rose wanted to tell her. There were advantages and disadvantages to this situation. One of the advantages being that it was summer, school was out so her father wasn't so hard-pressed about how she spent her free time. On the other hand, going anywhere or doing anything that didn't involve Janet meant she would have to explain herself. So, sneaking off wasn't going to work.

Unless Janet would agree to be her alibi, which also wouldn't work, seeing as how Janet didn't approve of Rose in the first place. This was going to be hard, but Darlene needed a plan by Saturday. She folded the paper and stuck it back under her mattress, with the necklace still around her neck, before falling asleep.

• • ᦂ • •

FOUR DAYS HAD PASSED, and it was the big day. Darlene finally had a plan. It wasn't perfect, but it was good enough to get her some time, possibly a few hours if necessary, but she wasn't counting on it.

She got dressed, tucking Rose's necklace inside of her undershirt. She wore something simple, a brown skirt that came to her knees, with a sky-blue top that buttoned to the top of her neck. She didn't want to look too dressed up, but she also didn't want to look like a rag doll in front of Rose. She tied her hair up, tightening it with a red ribbon. She hurried out of her room, kissing her grandma and father goodbye. She told them she was spending a few hours at Janet's house, which was a solid excuse, because they wouldn't expect her home until dinnertime.

The previous day, Darlene told Janet that she would be spending her Saturday helping Grandma Anne around the house, so she wouldn't be able to have company, or come to her house. This way, Janet wouldn't come to the house looking for her. It sounded like it would work and so far, no one was questioning anything, not even Darren. She hurried out the door and walked as fast as she could to make it to the Rosenberg's store by noon. Her heart was racing, and her palms were sweaty, not knowing what to expect when she got there. She wondered if Rose would even show up, and that made her even more nervous. Once again, she was not only putting herself at risk, but maybe even Rose. Or worse, getting her father in a lot of trouble. He worked for the Caldwell family, which should've been a good enough reason to end this little thing she was having with Rose. But it was too late. After the kiss, things would never be the same, even if Darlene wanted them to be.

When she approached the Rosenberg's store, she saw Rose's car. She took the pocket watch out of her pocket to check the time. It was almost noon. She felt a lump in her throat, but swallowed her fear, and proceeded to walk closer. Rose must have seen her in the rearview mirror, because she got out of the car before Darlene even approached it. Wearing brown pants, with a white sleeveless blouse, Darlene couldn't believe how stunning Rose looked. Her hair had even grown a few more inches, with her red wavy loose curls coming just under her earlobes and a little further down her neck. She had the right side of her hair tucked behind her ear. She didn't look as boyish as she did the last few times. She had a touch of femininity to her this time, and Darlene liked it...a lot. She approached Darlene with caution, hugged her the minute she got close enough.

"Hello," Rose said, in a soft voice. "I'm glad you came."

Chapter 13

THEY EMBRACED FOR A few seconds, before Darlene realized they were in public, in broad daylight, where people could still see them. She backed away.

"Well, I'm here. What did you want to talk about?" Darlene asked.

Rose noticed the necklace hidden underneath Darlene's shirt. "You're wearing my gift." She smiled, as she touched the necklace.

"Yes, I am. It's beautiful by the way, thank you." Darlene smiled. Rose's charming ways made Darlene forget for a second why she was there. She also realized that Rose hadn't answered her question.

"Rose, what do you want?"

"Let's get in my car; I want to take you somewhere."

"No! I can't go anywhere with you, I'm not even supposed to be here." She lowered her tone. "You said you wanted to tell me something. That's why I came." Darlene didn't want to be mean, but enough was enough.

"You want us to discuss it here? Out in the open, where people can see us? Wouldn't it be a better idea to go somewhere private?"

Darlene didn't want to admit it, but she had a point. She knew that whatever they were going to talk about wasn't something that should be discussed there. They were right outside the Rosenberg's store, which was risky enough.

"I can't get in trouble. You know that." Darlene told her.

"You won't. I promise."

Rose walked to the passenger's side and opened the door for Darlene. She hurried over and got inside. The quicker they could get out of there the better. Darlene pulled the necklace from under her shirt and twirled the sapphire sun with her fingers. Rose got in the driver's seat, started the car, and pulled away from the store, driving down the road. That red-haired girl with the mesmerizing grey eyes had done it again. For the third time, Darlene was in her car, breaking all the rules, and taking all the risks.

"So where are we going?" Darlene asked.

"My home."

"Your what?" Darlene stared at Rose like she was crazy. "No, Rose, I don't—"

"My parents are gone for the weekend. No one is there but our help, May. She won't say anything. Don't worry." Rose put Darlene's worries to rest, assuring her that she would be fine. "You trust me, don't you?"

"Yes, I do." Darlene spoke in a low voice, as if guilty for questioning Rose's trust.

"There is something I want to show you, too. I think you'll like it."

"Oh, is it another necklace?" Darlene sounded excited. "Another necklace? Don't tell me my girl is spoiled already?"

They both laughed.

My girl? Darlene wondered what Rose meant.

For a second, it sounded like Rose was insinuating the two were in a relationship. Like a boy-girl relationship. Except, neither one of them was a boy. Darlene was quiet for the remainder of the ride. Rose asked if she was okay, she nodded to let her know everything was fine. She didn't think Rose even realized what she had said. Or maybe she did, which is why she wanted to meet. Darlene wasn't sure she was ready for where this was going.

They pulled up to Rose's home, which was big, an eggshell white and beautiful—two stories, sitting on acres of bright green land. It was just as nice as she pictured it would be. Darlene had never been to a house this big before. She wasn't sure what to expect when she got inside. They got out the car, and Rose walked Darlene up to the front door. When Rose opened it, Darlene's eyes lit up like fireworks on the Fourth of July.

The smooth wooden floors, beautiful paintings hung on the walls; some were even of the family. Big displays of flowers sat on tiny little tables, and the smell, it was so welcoming. Darlene never wanted to leave.

"You haven't seen anything yet, follow me." Rose held out her hand and Darlene took it without hesitation. Rose's hands were soft, like creamy icing on a cake. They walked to the back of the house and Rose opened a door leading to the backyard. Darlene took a step outside and Rose was right. She hadn't seen anything yet. The garden was magnificent, with rows of tulips, lavenders, roses, daisies, and carnations, flowing so beautifully together.

Rose watched Darlene indulge in the beautiful view. "I knew you would love it."

Darlene ran down the small steps and rushed through the row of carnations, collapsing right in the middle of them. The aroma was breathtaking. Rose ran over to join her, plucking one of the carnations and lying down next to Darlene. She handed Darlene the flower, and Darlene held it up to her nose, taking in all the smells.

"This is wonderful." Darlene looked up at the sky. "You're so lucky to have this nice house and big garden. Your life is so great."

Rose looked over at Darlene. "It's all right. There is more to life than nice houses and gardens, ya know."

"That's easy for you to say when you have all this. It easy to think it's no big deal."

Offended by Darlene's remark, Rose left it alone. After all, Darlene was right. It's easy to have the mindset Rose did when you've never had to struggle for anything. Not that Darlene didn't agree, of course, in life there were more important things, which was why, despite her struggles being poor and black in the south, the bond of family was so strong. Material things didn't mean much to them, but at the same time, it was nice to get a taste of the "other side." The sapphire necklace, being in

Rose's home, in this garden; it was all new to Darlene and she had every right to compliment Rose's life.

Rose sat up, fingering her hair back behind her right ear. "So, about what I wanted to talk about."

Distracted by the beauty of Rose's home, Darlene forgot about that important conversation they needed to have. "Yeah..." She sat up to match Rose's posture.

"Have you ever felt like you were different than other girls?"

"What do you mean?"

"Like, different, as in how certain people make you feel."

Darlene got nervous about where this conversation was going. "I don't know." She broke eye contact with Rose.

"Well, I've known I was different for a very long time. Ever since I was a little kid." Rose paused, careful to choose the right words. "I like girls, Darlene. That's why I kissed you that night."

Darlene didn't know how to react to Rose's confession. This all became too overwhelming for her.

"Do you?" Rose asked.

Darlene couldn't speak. She had no idea how to answer, so she said the first thing that came to her mind. "I like you...a lot. I don't know what that means. I think my best friend Janet is really pretty, but I don't like her the same way I like you."

Rose smiled. "It means you like girls, too." She reached over and put her hand on Darlene's.

Darlene smiled, accepting Rose's embrace, as she now opened a whole new world that Darlene knew nothing about, outside of what she had heard at church.

"My pastor says girls aren't supposed to be with other girls. Or men with other men. It's against God's will."

"You believe that?" Rose asked.

"I don't know what I believe. I don't like to question God."

"Well, the heart never lies." Rose gripped Darlene's Darlene paused, taking a deep breath and gazing at the flowers.

"What took so long? Two months later, then you decide to send me a letter?"

"I didn't know how. I didn't know what to say, and I didn't think it was safe to come around, I thought you hated me." Rose had sadness in her voice.

"I could never hate you. I thought you hated me. The way you ran out afterwards."

"Of course, not."

"I thought about you all the time. I thought I'd never see you again."

Darlene's brown eyes looked into Roses eyes. Rose leaned in, caressed Darlene's chin, and kissed her on the lips. It was as magical as it was the first time. Only this time, no one was running away. It was perfect. In that moment, Darlene didn't even care if she liked girls, or boys, or if it was just Rose. It didn't matter. She found someone who made her feel beautiful and smart. Rose was understanding, sweet, funny, and unique.

In the middle of their kiss, Darlene noticed someone walking from inside the house, which startled her.

"Someone's coming!" She backed away from Rose, afraid that this person had witnessed everything.

Rose turned around. "It's May, the woman who works for my family. Don't worry."

They both stood up, trying to pretend nothing had happened. May walked further out, getting closer to them and using her hand to block the sun from her eyes so she could see clearly.

"Rose, I didn't know you were home. You have a friend?" Her eyes turned to Darlene. "Hello, Miss."

"Hi." Darlene greeted with hesitation.

"May, this is my friend, Darlene. I was just showing her the garden." Rose explained.

"I don't mean to disturb, my apologies, Miss." Said May.

"It's fine, May, we'll be going back inside now anyway." Rose patted May on the shoulder, her way of reassuring her that it really wasn't an issue, so she shouldn't apologize. May led both girls back into the house, where she proceeded to finish her cleaning tasks.

"Do you think she saw anything?" Darlene whispered.

"I don't think so. Even if she did, she wouldn't say anything to my parents, so there's nothing to worry about." Rose assured her.

Darlene grinned, holding Rose's hand. She was having the most amazing day, and she was too busy enjoying her time with Rose to be worried about getting into trouble. She felt free, and it was the best feeling she had ever had.

Chapter 14

ROSE LED DARLENE TO the staircase. "You want to go to my room and listen to my records?"

"I love music." Darlene said excitedly. Her family didn't have a record player. The only time she could listen to music was at Janet's house, and that was only when her mother allowed it.

Rose and Darlene walked up the stairs and into Rose's room. It was spacious, but simple. Rose clearly wasn't one for fancy décor, which was obvious. There were no photos, just a painting of a dark human figure, fishing in a lake, with a sunset. The only hint of femininity in her bedroom was the white waterfall vanity, and the flowerpot Darlene had given her, which was sitting next to the mirror. Based on Rose's style choices, Darlene could tell Rose didn't use the vanity often. Not that it needed to be, Rose was stunning without the extra work.

Rose walked over to her record player and grabbed a record from the top of her stack. She decided to play *Sing Sing Sing* by Benny Goodman. Walking over to Darlene, she extended her hand, asking for a dance. Without saying a word, Darlene accepted by grabbing Rose's hand and moving in closer.

"Have you ever danced with anyone before?" Rose guided Darlene in circles.

"No." Darlene was trying to keep up without stepping on Roses toes. It was true. She had never danced at all. "My momma and daddy used to dance a lot, before she died. I would watch them."

"Do you remember her much?"

"A little." Darlene thought about her mother. The little memories she had left. "She loved flowers, just like me. She was always happy. Her and Daddy. He smiled and laughed a lot back then. He hardly ever laughs anymore." It was true, Mr. Jones hadn't been the same since he lost his wife.

The memories of her parents' old life together made her sad. Rose could tell, so she decided to stop asking questions and let them both enjoy the moment.

"What are your parents like?"

Rose let out a huge sigh. "Well, my mother, she really riles me up sometimes. We used to be very close when I was little. Then as I got older, I started to change—or so she said. We just drifted apart after that."

Darlene had a hard time empathizing with her. Rose had a mother, who was alive and well, and she acted as if she wanted nothing to do with her. Surley, a strict mother was better than no mother at all.

"My dad, well he's not as bad as my mother. Not when it comes to me, anyway. He's a good man with a good heart; I just wish he'd treat others better. People who aren't rich or White."

Darlene assessed Rose was nothing like her parents. She was like an orchid growing around crab grass. The more Darlene learned about Rose, the more she pitied her.

"I don't want to talk about them anymore." Rose ended that conversation.

The song ended, and Rose released Darlene and walked back over to her record player to put on something else. She wanted to keep the mood going, so she played *Jeepers Creepers* by Louis Armstrong.

"Oh, I like this song! It's me and Janet's favorite!"

As she sang along with the lyrics, Rose walked over to her bed and grabbed her pack of smokes she kept hidden. Pulling one out and lighting it with a match, Darlene looked at her in surprise. Rose glanced back at her and laughed.

"You want one?"

"One of those? No thanks, I'm not supposed to smoke."

"Well, you're not supposed to be here with me either, yet, here you are." Rose puffed her cigarette. She playfully mocked Darlene. Although it was annoying, that whimsical personality was one of the many reasons she found Rose attractive.

"Give me that." Darlene grabbed the box of smokes. She put one in her mouth and lit the end, taking her first puff. It was good, in an odd kind of way. Her throat felt heavy, probably from all the excessive coughing.

"Are you okay?" Rose got worried, even though she thought it was a bit funny.

"I'm fine," arlene uttered between coughs.

Darlene took a seat on the bed next to Rose. She was still puffing the cigarette. She didn't love it, but she didn't hate it enough to stop. This was probably why her father told her to never try it.

"Do your parents know?"

"Yeah. I told them I would stop, but they know I still smoke. They just like to pretend that they don't."

Darlene stopped taking puffs from her cigarette and faced Rose. "That's not what I meant."

"No, my parents don't know I like girls. As much as my mother scolds me about my appearance and love life, I don't think she even has a clue. My father is so busy with work, he doesn't notice anything."

Rose's secret ate her up inside. She couldn't fathom telling her parents about who she really was. It hurt every time she played the scenario of coming out to them in her head, which was one of the reasons she still smoked.

Rose was hurting, that much Darlene could tell. She rested her head on Rose's shoulder, wanting to comfort her. She thought about what it would be like if she told her father and grandmother something like that. There was no way in hell, not even if hell froze over. Both girls sat there, quiet, taking in the sounds of the music playing.

"I just want to get out of here. Go to the big city and live my dream." Rose said.

"Why don't you? Your family is rich. I'm sure they can just give you money."

"No, they don't support my dreams. My mother wants me to be a wife and mother, mincing around a big house all day long, like she does. My father wants me to do the same, or if I'm so determined to be a working woman, I should work with money. Become a banker or something."

"So, what will you do then?" Darlene felt sorry for her, as her father didn't put those kinds of demands on her life.

"I don't know. Just sit around with you, fishing, smoking cigarettes, and admiring the smell of Begonia's in a field?" Rose nudged Darlene's shoulder.

Darlene smiled, knowing Rose was only joking. She was used to her humor by now.

"I want to be a doctor. I don't think it'll happen, but it would be nice." Darlene said.

"You can be whatever you want."

"No, *you* can be whatever you want. I'm not like you. We're not the same, you know that." Darlene said.

"That doesn't mean anything. I believe in you." Rose tried to be endearing but it wasn't working.

Darlene had lost interest in the topic of careers. As sweet as Rose was, her denial of her own privilege was annoying.

"I should be going soon." As much as she didn't want to leave, Darlene knew she couldn't stay too much longer.

"Couldn't you stay a little while longer?" Rose didn't want her time with Darlene to end so soon.

Darlene gazed into Rose's lonely eyes. In a matter of months, Darlene went from being shy, insecure, and uncertain about her own place in this world, to something so much better. With Rose, she was carefree, confident, and happy. Yes, she was happy at home, but this was a different type of joy. A new joy. She moved in closer, caressing the smooth skin on Rose's face with her fingertips. Darlene kissed her on the lips, and they were just as soft as they were when she kissed her in the garden. Rose touched Darlene's face, running her thumb over her perfectly shaped eyebrows, admiring Darlene's beauty with every passing second. The girls spent the next half hour swapping stories, bonding over their favorite songs, until they heard a knock at the door. It was May.

"Rose, dear, can I get you and your guest anything?" May asked, from the other side of the door.

"No thank you, May. We are just fine." Rose told her.

"All right now, Miss Rose." May went back to doing her daily house tasks.

Darlene took May's disruption as a sign that it was time to leave. "I should really be going now." Darlene passed Rose her cigarette.

Rose smashed their cigarettes in a nearby ashtray. They stood up. Rose removed the record from the player, placing it back with the rest, and both girls left the room. As they walked back downstairs, May was wiping the windows in the sitting room when she turned to look at Darlene. Darlene smiled.

"It was nice to meet you, Ms. May." Darlene said politely.

May didn't say anything. She turned away and continued on with her cleaning task. Darlene was surprised that May ignored her gesture. It was odd, because she seemed so nice earlier.

"We'll be going now, May. I'll be back later."

"All right now Miss Rose."

Darlene felt disrespected. May had deliberately brushed off her politeness and only acknowledged Rose. Darlene didn't want to make a fuss about it to Rose, who didn't seem to notice. So she just let it go.

As they were walking out the door, Darlene turned around, getting one last look at May, who had glanced back at her, before turning back around to tend to her cleaning, again. It was strange. She wondered why this woman seemed so apprehensive towards her, as if she were an alien or a criminal. Darlene then thought back to the garden. She thought that maybe May saw her and Rose kiss after all. Even then, why was she only acting that way toward Darlene and not Rose? They got into Rose's car and Darlene got one last look at the beautiful house before they drove away.

They arrived at the same spot where Rose had dropped Darlene off the previous times they had spent time together.

Rose stopped the car, and she and Darlene sat in silence for a few seconds before Rose spoke.

"I had a great time with you today."

"Me, too." For Darlene, saying goodbye was a solemn moment.

"We'll see each other again, don't worry." Rose grabbed Darlene's hand.

"I still have a while before I'll be back in school, maybe you can come over for dinner again? Or maybe you can take me to the lake again?"

"Maybe." Rose put on a phony smile, trying to be optimistic.

She knew that she and Darlene would have a hard time maintaining their relationship, especially if things were going to be more serious. She couldn't bring Darlene around her parents, or Ricky. As much as she cared for her, they could never really be together as they wanted to be. This realization made it even harder to part.

"A week, give me a week, and you'll hear from me again. I promise, and this time, I won't make you sneak away." Rose assured her.

Darlene leaned over, giving Rose one last kiss, this time on the cheek, before getting out of the car.

"One week? Pinky swear?" Darlene smiled.

"Promise."

Darlene walked away, trying to hurry back home before Grandma started preparing for dinner. Rose watched her leave before driving away. The entire walk to her house, Darlene couldn't stop thinking about their afternoon together. She wanted to tell Janet so badly that she saw Rose again, but at the same time, possessing the secret made it much more exciting. As she approached her house, her father was sitting on the porch steps. Her first reaction was to go up and give him the usual hugs and kisses, but then as she got closer she noticed an expression on his face that made her stomach turn. She also noticed a piece of paper in his hands. This didn't feel good.

"Daddy..."

She then noticed Darren walking out of the house, giving her a look of disgust. She then looked back at the paper her father was holding. Her heart stopped and her whole world felt dark. It was the letter from Rose.

Oh no.

Chapter 15

"DADDY, WAIT, I CAN explain!" Darlene slowly approached her father. She was terrified. She had no idea how to explain this to her family. As he was approaching the steps, Darren came down the steps to confront her.

"I knew it! The way you were looking at her that night at dinner, on the porch! How odd you had been acting, it was all because of her!" He shouted. "After I found your little letter, daddy went to Janet's to find you, and she told us everything!"

"Darnell, I..."

"You're a lesbian! That's why you don't like Walter, or any of the boys at school, isn't it?" Darren was still shouting at his sister.

Darlene was crying. She hadn't even had the time to wrap her head around what was going on. It was all unraveling so fast, she felt like she was going to vomit.

"Get away from her, boy!" Mr. Jones interrupted. He got up from the steps, with the paper crumpled up in his hand.

Grandma Anne appeared in the doorway, with concern in her eyes. "Joe, don't!" Grandma Anne called out from behind the screen door.

Joe smacked Darlene across the face. It was loud and painful. Even Darnell had a look of shock on his face from what his father had just done.

"Joe, you didn't have to do that!" Grandma Anne
yelled.

"Shut up and go back inside, Annie!"

Darlene was holding her face where her father had struck her, tears still rolling down her face.

"What is this?" he demanded between clenched teeth and seething anger. "You going around kissing girls now?

Rose!" He was furious. "You need to explain this and explain it now!" He held up the crumpled letter. He wrinkled his nose. "And, what is that smell? Have you been smoking?"

Still crying, Darlene tried to gather her words to speak. "We—We're friends. That's all," she stuttered.

"Friends! This letter don't sound like friends to me!" he barked. He grabbed Rose's necklace that Darlene was wearing around her neck. "This. That's why she gave you this expensive necklace. Take it off, now!"

"No!" Darlene shouted, as she grabbed the necklace, in fear that her father would yank it from her neck.

Mr. Jones was in shock. He felt like he was staring into the eyes of a girl he didn't know. His mind was still trying to process the fact that his daughter had been running around with not only a stranger, but a White stranger, and out of all people, Rose. Even though she wasn't a stranger to him, his daughter hadn't known at the time, which made it no better. On top of all of that, his daughter was a lesbian? He had no more words.

"Get out of my sight. I can't even look at you."

There was more pain in his voice than anger that much Darlene could tell. She looked to her grandmother for help, whose tear-filled eyes watched the humiliation of her granddaughter by her father in front of their home. Darlene could tell by the look on Grandma Anne's face that, even though she wanted to, it was best for her not to intervene.

Darren had walked back into the house, shaking his head in disgust.

"Daddy, please don't do this."

Mr. Jones turned around and walked back into the house, slamming the door behind him, leaving his daughter outside.

Still in shock by what had taken place, Darlene had no one else to turn to, besides Janet. So, she ran to her best friend's house, who she was hoping wouldn't turn her away.

Once she arrived at Janet's house, she stood on the steps for a few seconds, replaying the events that had just happened with her family in her head. A part of her wanted to knock, and another part of her didn't. After all, Janet had told Darren and her father everything about Rose. Darlene wanted to be angry, but knew Janet had no choice. At the end of the day, Janet was just looking out for her friend.

Darlene mustered up her courage to knock on the door, while wiping tears from her wet face. Janet's mother opened the door.

"Hello, Darlene," she paused at the sight of Darlene's bruised face. "Oh, what's wrong?" It was obvious she had been crying too. "Your father and brother were looking for you. Are you all right?"

"I'm fine, Ma'am. May I see Janet, please?" Darlene tried to hide the pain in her voice.

"Yes, come in."

Ms. Benson stood to the side, allowing Darlene to enter. Janet was coming toward the door as Darlene was walking in. She saw Darlene's face and knew there was trouble. Janet ran to her, giving her a big hug.

"Oh my, God, Darlene, what happened? You were with Rose, weren't you? I'm sorry; I told your father everything! I had to, we were all worried!" Janet's voice held a combination of fear, disappointment, and relief.

"Janet, I can't go back home. Daddy hates me."

Janet's eyes grew big. "What do you mean? What happened to you?" Janet touched the bruise on Darlene's face.

"Daddy and Darren found a letter that Rose wrote to me. I was with her this afternoon. When I got home, Daddy was angry. He hit me and told me to leave."

Ms. Benson gasped, with her hands over her mouth. "Oh no, I'm so sorry, Darlene! You can stay here for as long as you like. Right, Momma?" Janet turned toward her mother for clarification.

"Yes, yes you may. I'll go get a warm cloth for your face." Ms. Benson walked off, and Janet walked Darlene to her room.

"I'm sorry, Darlene, I really am. I shouldn't have told them anything. When they came here looking for you, I realized that you were with her. I was angry and hurt that you lied again. I'm sorry."

"It's not your fault, I shouldn't have lied to you. I'm not mad at you for telling them. I know you were only looking out for me."

Ms. Benson came to Janet's room with the cloth to tend to Darlene's face. "Just hold that there for a bit, you should be fine." She walked out of the room, letting the girls talk.

Janet noticed the necklace around Darlene's neck. Her eyes widened in shock. "What in heavens name is this? It looks so expensive!" Janet grabbed the necklace.

"Rose gave it to me, for my birthday."

"That girl gave you this?" Janet was as confused and surprised as Darlene's family was the night they saw it. "But you hardly know her. Why would she give you something so... expensive? I don't understand..."

Darlene had no idea how to explain any of this to her, or even if she should. The damage was done, but the last thing she wanted to do was lose her friend.

"Me and Rose... We're... good friends now. Daddy doesn't like it. He says I can't be friends with her because she's White." Darlene knew it was best to avoid the major intimate details of her and Rose's relationship. She knew Janet would find out eventually and would possibly be hurt again by Darlene's lack of honesty, but right now, she just couldn't. If Darlene's own family couldn't handle it, how could Janet?

"Well, the necklace really is pretty." Janet tried to lighten the mood.

"I just want to sleep." Darlene was exhausted by the evening's events.

"I'll go get more blankets."

Janet left to grab a blanket for Darlene, while Darlene sat on Janet's bed, with the warm cloth still on her cheek.

Church was tomorrow. But there was no way Darlene was showing her face there. She was suffering in her own sins enough. The last thing she needed was for them to be on display in front of the entire church. She had no idea how she could face her family again. She knew she couldn't hide at Janet's house forever. Rose would know what to do, she thought. But that wasn't an option. After today, she had no idea what this would mean for her and Rose's relationship, or her father's job. Everything was falling apart.

Chapter 16

THE NEXT MORNING, DARLENE had awakened to Ms. Benson and Janet returning from church. She was still snuggled under the blanket, contemplating on where to go from here, physically and emotionally. Before she went to bed the night before, she had a million scenarios go through her head of what church would be like. If her father or brother would say anything to anyone, of if Pastor Lee would ban her from church. What about her family? Being a part of the church was the least of her worries, but she would never forgive herself if her family, especially Grandma Anne, could never return because of her actions. She heard footsteps coming toward the room, so she turned over to Janet opening the door.

"Is it true?"

By the tone of her voice, Darlene knew she wasn't ready to answer that question.

"Huh?" Darlene pretended as if she didn't understand.

"You and that White girl! Is it true? Darren told me!" Janet yelled, with tears in her eyes.

Darlene couldn't tell if they were tears of anger or pain. It didn't matter. Darlene got out of bed, throwing the blanket to the opposite side of the bed. She looked at her best friend, not knowing what to say, but knowing it was time to be honest.

"It is."

They both had the exact same look of shock on their faces, Janet probably more shocked than Darlene. Janet's jaw dropped. She didn't know how to process it.

"I know. I'm just as confused as you are, and I can't believe I just said that. I don't know what my brother told you, but I'm going to tell you the truth. Me and Rose became closer than I led on. We started having feelings toward each other, and I didn't understand them at first. The night she came to my house for dinner, we kissed. I didn't see her again until yesterday. We wanted to talk about what happened, and that's when we realized that we care about each other. Not like how you and I do, but like, how men and women do."

While Darlene was explaining all of this, Janet's facial expression hadn't changed at all. There was a moment of silence. Darlene waited to see what Janet would say or do. She couldn't believe that she not only admitted her true feelings to her best friend, but to herself —that she was in love with Rose. She smiled.

Janet finally spoke, after minutes of submergence in her own emotions. "I don't know who you are anymore." She couldn't even look at Darlene.

"Janet, I know this is a lot to hear, but—"

"I think you should leave." Janet didn't even let Darlene finish her sentence.

Darlene was hurt, her eyes filled with tears. She was expecting to hear many things, but not that. Anger, confusion, even fear she expected, but abandonment hurt worst of all. If Janet wanted her to leave, where would she go? She had no one, but Rose, who she had no way of contacting. Darlene stood up and walked toward Janet.

"But Janet, I have nowhere else to go."

Janet stepped back as Darlene moved closer toward her. "Go back home then. But you can't stay here anymore. You need to leave." The pain in Janet's voice was clear. Her heart didn't want to abandon her best friend, but she felt like she had no choice.

Ms. Benson had been listening from the door and made her way to Janet's room. She didn't say anything, just stood with her arms crossed, looking at Darlene with disgust, and disappointment. Darlene knew that this meant she needed to leave now. Crying, Darlene made her way toward the front door of the house, looking back at Janet and Ms. Benson one last time, before leaving. Once she reached the porch, she ran. She didn't know where she was running to, but she knew she couldn't stop. Not until she got far enough away from everyone and everything. As she ran, she passed by people walking, working, carrying on with their daily lives and felt like every single pair of eyes were on her. All she felt was shame. She kept running until she got to the Rosenberg's store. The memory of meeting up with Rose flashed through her mind, which felt like a lifetime ago even though it was just yesterday. She didn't know what else to do but run inside.

She opened the door and the bell jingled. She waited for someone to come. Thankfully, the store seemed to be empty, which was good. The last thing Darlene wanted right now was an audience. A few seconds later, Christopher appeared from the isle, greeting her as he usually did. He had his hands full of bags of flour, one leaking onto the floor, as he stumbled over to Darlene.

"Hello, Darlene, can I get something for you? You look swell today!" he said in a cheerful, yet nervous voice.

Darlene didn't say anything, but her eyes and face were still wet from crying. Christopher noticed and became concerned.

"Darlene, are you all right? You look upset."

She still said nothing but cried again. Christopher dropped the bags and touched Darlene's shoulder. "Come with me."

He turned the sign hanging on the door from open to close, so they could have some privacy. He led her to the back, and they sat down on wooden crates.

He noticed the bruise from where her father hit her. "Your face! Are you in trouble?"

Darlene wiped her face and looked at Christopher. "Where is your mom?" She asked.

"Huh? Oh, my mother went to Asheville for a few days to visit my uncle. I'm looking after the store while she's gone."

He didn't want to talk about his mother; he wanted to know why Darlene was upset.

"Darlene, what's wrong? Can I help?" He was eager for her to answer him.

"My father is mad at me. So is Janet. I can't explain why right now, but I don't have anywhere to go. I can't go home. I just came here. I don't know why." She cried.

Christopher put his hand on her shoulder to comfort her. He didn't know what to say. He knew it wasn't polite to ask for details since it was none of his business to pry.

"You can stay here. We have a spare room upstairs. My mother will be gone until Thursday, so you can stay here until then, at least."

Darlene's eyes lit up with surprise. Although she had come to the store seeking some type of emotional aid, she wasn't expecting him to offer for her to stay. Not that she was in any position to decline. At that moment, all she could do was hug him. She had known Christopher and his mother since her family had moved to town. They had never shared more than a few hellos and goodbyes, smiles and waves, and he was giving her shelter without knowing so much as her name. He was the calm in the middle of her storm.

"Christopher, I don't know how to thank you."

"You don't have to thank me. I just want to help."

He led her upstairs. The Rosenberg's lived above their store. They had three small bedrooms, and a kitchen. It was quite cozy, given how small it was. The spare bedroom had nothing but a bed and a little table across from it with a lamp. Darlene sat down while Christopher went to his room, returning a few minutes later with a set of clothes and a blanket.

"You can change into these, if you want." He sat the shirt and pants next to her.

"Thank you."

He turned on the lamp before leaving the room, closing the door slowly behind him, and heading back downstairs.

Darlene pulled the necklace Rose had given her from under her shirt, twirling it with her fingers before taking it off and laying it on the little table. She also still had the pocket watch her father had given her for her birthday. She had nearly forgotten about it. She sat that next to it, then turned the lamp off, and got in bed, lying flat on her back, looking up at the ceiling. She thought about the events of the past two days and how her life had changed within the blink of an eye. For the first time in her young life, she literally felt nothing but darkness.

Chapter 17

IT WAS TUESDAY MORNING, and Rose sat on her porch, smoking her cigarette as usual. She was in the best mood she had been in, in a very long time. She was daydreaming about her time with Darlene, thinking about the next time they could get together. She was planning to stop by Darlene's house, and asking Mr. Joe if they could go fishing at the lake. It was a bold move, but what reasons would he have to say no? He liked Rose and was the one who wanted them to get to know each other when she came for dinner. Well now, they were friends. More than friends, but that was more than he needed to know. Rose figured it was a good plan, and Darlene wouldn't have to sneak around anymore. Mr. Caldwell storming out of the house, fuming mad, interrupted her daydreaming.

"This is unacceptable!" Mr. Caldwell yelled.

Rose hadn't seen her father this angry in a while. She looked at her watch and realized it was forty-three minutes past seven. Mr. Joe was late. That's why her father was angry. Joe had been late before, but not in a while.

"Second day in a row this man neglects his job! I guess I'll just have to drive myself then!" Mr. Caldwell yelled, making his way to the car, with his hat clenched in one hand and briefcase in the other.

Rose had spent the previous day with Ricky, so she hadn't noticed that Mr. Joe hadn't shown up for work. If this was his second day not showing up, then something must've been wrong. He was a hardworking man who wouldn't just abandon his job like that.

"Maybe he's sick?" Rose tried to convince her father as she followed him to the car.

"Sick or not, he has a responsibility to be here! Since you're so concerned about his wellbeing, you can tell him he's fired if he decides to show up!"

Mr. Caldwell pulled away without saying another word.

Rose couldn't believe her father was being so cruel. Now she was worried and felt as though she had to go see what was going on. This was also a good excuse to see Darlene. She smashed her cigarette with her foot, and walked over to her car, got in and pulled off just as quickly as her father did. During the drive, she thought about what her father said. There was no way she could tell Mr. Joe to his face that he had just lost his job. The idea of doing that made her stomach turn. It would crush him, and not only that, there was no way Darlene would forgive her for it.

She pulled up to the Jones' house and saw that Mr. Joe's car was still there. She got out and made her way to the door. After only knocking once, Darren answered the door.

"What are you doing here?" Darren said angrily through clenched teeth. He walked toward her, causing her to take a few steps back.

"Your father, he didn't come in to work today, I just wanted to make sure he was okay," Rose said, being cautious with her words.

"Did you? Or did you come here for my sister?"

Caught off guard, Rose didn't know how to answer.

"We know what you are." Darren looked at her with disgust.

Rose felt her entire body go numb. She couldn't believe what was happening. They knew. They knew everything. About her, about Darlene...but how? She stood with her mouth wide open.

"Get away from my home. You disgust me. You and her!" Darren yelled.

Before Rose could even muster up any kind of response, Mr. Joe came walking out from behind Darren. He gently pushed his son aside, so he could see her. He looked like he hadn't slept in days. With the bags under his eyes, and the cripple in his walk, the toll that all of this was taking on him was obvious.

"What are you doing here, Rose? Why are you at my house?" His voice was hoarse. He didn't even call her Rosie, as he always had. Just Rose, as if she were a stranger. Darren was still standing behind his father, defensive, his eyes locked dead on Rose.

"I just wanted to see if you were all right. You didn't come into work." Rose said.

"I'm not coming back to work for your family anymore."

Rose couldn't believe what she was hearing. Somehow, it hurt worse than having to tell him he no longer had a job. She knew it was because of her and Darlene. Guilt overwhelmed her. She could feel it in her stomach.

"Mr. Joe, you can't! You need this job! What about your family? What about Darlene?"

"My family, and especially my daughter, is none of your concern. I know about you two. I saw the letter you wrote my daughter. I always had a feeling you were different, Rose, but it was none of my business. But now you got my daughter involved in this mess of sin. I want nothing to do with it, her, you, or your family."

Rose was hurt. She wanted to defend herself, and Darlene, but knew it was best to say nothing.

"I need you to leave now." He turned around to walk away, beginning to close the door when Rose put her hand in to stop him.

"Where is she? Where is Darlene?" Rose asked.

"I don't know. But you won't find her here. So, don't come back. Goodbye, Miss Rosie." He went back inside without saying another word.

Rose and Darren were now face-to-face. He knew better than to try anything, but he was still angry. Rose wasn't afraid of him but knew the best thing to do was leave before she caused their family any more trouble. Besides, she had to find Darlene. She walked away from the door and proceeded to get into her car. She tried to think of how she could find Darlene. She didn't know any of her friends and couldn't exactly go around a Negro town asking questions. She clenched the wheel, frustrated, until she remembered the Rosenberg's store. The least she could do is ask if they've seen her, which was better than not doing anything. Darren stood at the door, watching Rose until she drove away.

She drove until she reached the store, and without even bothering to park, she got out of her car and ran inside. Christopher was sweeping near the counter. Startled by her entrance, he dropped his broom.

"Can I help you, Miss?"

"Hi, my name is Rose. I didn't mean to barge in like that. I'm sorry." She walked over and picked up his broom for him. "I'm looking for someone. Her name is Darlene. She lives nearby, and I'm sure she comes here often. I was wondering if you've seen her."

Christopher became curious as to why this girl was looking for Darlene. It was strange, especially considering Darlene had come to the store so distraught. He wasn't sure what Rose wanted but wasn't going to give up Darlene so easily.

"Why would you be looking for her?" He asked, not trying to sound too suspicious.

"So, you do know her?"

"I do, yes. Her and her family are regulars here." "Well, have you seen her? It's important."

Christopher knew it was a good idea to talk to Darlene before telling Rose anything. "Will you excuse me for a moment? I have some quick business to take care of. You caught me at a busy time. Just give me a moment, please."

He sat his broom against the counter and went upstairs to get Darlene. When he approached the room, he gently knocked and asked her permission to come in.

"Come in."

When he opened the door, Darlene was reading a book he had given her to keep her busy. She closed it and sat it beside her on the bed.

"There is a girl downstairs. A White girl. With red hair. She's asking about you."

Darlene's eyes lit up. She couldn't believe Rose was there.

"Rose? She's here?" Her tone of voice was more surprised than excited. She wasn't expecting to see Rose ever again, and there she was, waiting downstairs.

"So, you do know her?"

"Yes. She's... a friend. It's all right," Darlene said softly.

"Well, if she wants to talk to you, I think it's best that you talk up here. Just in case I get any customers. I'll send her up."

Christopher still wasn't sure about what was going on, but just as a precaution, he didn't want Darlene and Rose causing any type of unnecessary attention if anyone came in. He closed the door partially and walked back downstairs to get Rose. Darlene ran her hands through her hair, which had become bushy and untamed. She realized she was wearing Christopher's clothes, but didn't care. Seeing Rose was more important than her appearance. She heard footsteps coming toward the door. She stood up. Rose walked in and smiled. They smiled at each other, and Darlene didn't waste any time running over to hug her. Their smiles turned to frowns as they both realized that this was not a happy reunion.

"My family, they know. They know everything. My friend, Janet, too. It was horrible. My father hit me." Darlene was crying.

Rose didn't even notice the bruise until Darlene mentioned it.

"My God. How could he do that?" Rose caressed the bruise on Darlene's face.

"Did my father say anything to you when he went to work?"

Rose then remembered her encounter with Mr. Joe at his house. She had to tell Darlene.

"I went to your house, before I came here. Your father didn't show up for work yesterday or today. I was worried, so I came by to check on him."

Darlene's eyes grew big with worry. "He missed work? Oh no, it's all because of me!"

"He told me that he wasn't coming back to work for us anymore. I asked him where you were, and he told me that he didn't know. He was upset."

"He quit his job because of us," Darlene uttered. The guilt had multiplied. "I can't go back home anyway. Everyone hates me. I didn't know where to go, so I came here, and Christopher is letting me stay for a few days."

"I'm going to get you out of here." Rose grabbed Darlene's shoulders.

"To go where?"

"Anywhere. If your family wants to treat you this way, then forget them!"

"Forget them? I can't just forget them. Even if they hate me, they're my family."

"You don't need them, you have me. That's all that matters now."

Taken aback by Rose's harsh tone, Darlene snapped, "No, no, that's not all that matters now." She paced the room. "What am I supposed to do now if I can't go back to my family? What is my family supposed to do if my father lost his job?"

"There will always be other jobs, Darlene, they'll be fine. We'll be fine."

"No, we won't be fine! It won't be fine! You don't get it, do you?" Darlene's voice filled with passion and anger.

"What am I not getting? Why are you angry with me? I'm not the problem here. We're in this together, remember?"

At that moment, it was as if everything had flashed before Darlene's eyes. Her and Rose were two completely different people, with com-

pletely different lives. Both stuck in a situation with separate consequences. She was taking shelter in a little room above a store. Possibly
an outcast from everything and everyone she had ever known, while
Rose wanted to drive off into the sunset together. Darlene's life, as she
knew it, was over, and Rose was living in a fairytale of privilege.

"But, you are the problem," Darlene said to her, backing away to sit
on the bed. "From the moment you told me to get into your car the
first time, you became the problem. The day you approached me out of
nowhere, to go to the lake with you, you became the problem. The moment you came to my house with my father, and stayed even when you
saw me, knowing that it wasn't a good idea, you became the problem!

Then we kissed, and I honestly wished you never wrote me that letter or gave me that necklace."

Crushed, Rose hated hearing Darlene say these things. She walked
over to sit on the bed next to her. "Why are you saying these things?
Where is all of this coming from?"

"This isn't a fantasy, this is my life. You're White and rich. The
world is your oyster. This isn't all there is for you. Your parents don't
even know about us, or about what you are."

"So?" Rose replied with a snarky tone.

"That's exactly what I mean, you don't care! You go through life
careless about everything! You don't care how your actions affect the
people you care about because you don't have to! I know I screwed up,
and I must suffer for it. But you're delusional, self-absorbed, and blind-
ed by your own selfishness!"

They were interrupted by Christopher, who had been eaves dropping. "Is everything all right in here, Darlene?" He tried not to make it
obvious that he had been snooping.

"We're fine. Rose will be leaving in a sec." Darlene told him.

Christopher walked back downstairs, and Rose got up to close the
door. She was confused as to why Darlene was treating her this way. She

loved her, and wanted nothing more than to help her, yet Darlene was treating her as if she were the enemy. It was painful.

"Darlene, I know you're upset, but you've got to trust me. I care about you more than I've ever cared about anyone. I just want us to be together."

Darlene walked over to the table. She picked up the necklace Rose had given her, admiring the sapphire with her fingertips.

"I care about you, too. But, what we're doing it isn't right."

"I thought being different didn't matter to you? I thought you came to terms with what we are?"

"What we are? I'm not talking about that. I'm talking about the lying, hurting our friends and families, it's not right. But just to be clear, I never said I was anything. You did."

Darlene walked over to Rose. She extended her hand, the necklace resting in her palm. Rose took her hand and pushed it back.

"It's yours. I won't take it back. I don't care if you sell it, or throw it away, but I won't take it back, and I won't let you just walk away from this." Rose wasn't giving up without a fight.

Darlene knew it was time. Time to move on. As much as she cared for Rose, this couldn't go on any longer. Their feelings for each other couldn't mend the damage. She felt God had made it clear, that although meeting Rose was no mistake, nothing good would come of them continuing to see each other. It hurt, but it was how things had to be, especially if there was any chance of her getting her family and Janet back. She leaned in toward Rose and kissed her. It bought back memories of that day in her room, when they kissed for the first time. It was as if they were replaying that exact moment over again, standing in front of each other, near the door, without a care in the world.

Chapter 18

"I'M COMING BACK TOMORROW, and I'm taking you out of here. Don't worry about where or how." Rose caressed Darlene's cheek. "I promise, everything will be better tomorrow."

"I know." Darlene had no intentions on being there tomorrow.

"See you then."

Darlene didn't respond, she just nodded. Rose had her hand on the doorknob for a few seconds, as if she were reluctant to leave. Darlene was afraid that Rose could tell exactly what she was thinking.

"I really am sorry, you know," Rose uttered.

"I know." Darlene was trying to hold back tears. "I'll see you tomorrow, okay? Go get yourself ready and I'll be here waiting for you."

Rose left, without saying another word, closing the door behind her.

Darlene took a deep breath, making her way back to the bed, emotionally drained. Rose would come back, looking for her but she would be gone. She didn't know where she would go, but it wasn't going to be with Rose. Christopher knocked on the door, coming to check on her.

"You can come in, it's fine." Darlene told him.

He opened the door and walked over to her, sitting next to her on the bed. "I don't mean to pry, but are you all right?"

"I'm okay. Thanks for asking, and thanks for allowing me to stay here." Darlene took another deep breath before continuing. "I'm leaving tomorrow. I don't know where to exactly, but I'll figure it out."

Christopher didn't like the idea of her being out on her own. While he was listening in on her conversation with Rose, he knew enough to know that she was in desperate need of help. He couldn't let her leave tomorrow with nowhere to go.

"I have an uncle, Peter. He lives in Asheville. He has a farm. You can go there. I'm sure he'll be willing to give you a job. He's always looking for new help. I'm his only nephew, he'd do anything for me, and that includes helping out a friend."

Darlene was surprised by his offer. She didn't think he was serious. She couldn't possibly go all the way to Asheville. Then again, she was about to run away, with nowhere to go, so this didn't sound any crazier than the sleeping alone on the streets.

"Oh, Christopher, I couldn't—"

"It's all right. He's a good man, he won't mind that you're a Negro, either, if that's what you're worried about."

"How would I even get there? I don't have a car, or any money. What about my family?"

"You can always come back, I'm sure your family will understand. I can take you to Asheville, if you want to go. It's really up to you."

Darlene didn't even have to think twice. She had a way out, and she was going to take it.

"Okay. I'll go."

Christopher smiled with relief. "I'm glad. Can you be ready tonight? I think its best we leave after nightfall. It's safer, for the both of us."

Tonight? It seemed so sudden. "Yes, I can."

He nodded in agreeance with her decision, and left the room in a hurry, going back downstairs in case there were customers waiting. Darlene walked over to the desk to pick up the book she had been reading before Rose arrived. She sat the necklace back in its place and got back in bed. She felt like everything would be okay. She didn't know Christopher that well, but she trusted his word. He was kind, and she could tell that his heart was full of good intentions. Even if she were having second thoughts about this plan to go to Asheville, it's not as if she had any other choices. This was her opportunity at a second chance. Maybe in a few months, she could come back and rekindle her relationships with her family and Janet. Just because they were angry, didn't mean she no longer loved them. She would at least leave them notes, telling them not to worry, or to look for her.

Right before it was time to leave, she had gone downstairs to ask Christopher for something to write with and paper. She told him she would be leaving the notes with him to give to her family and Janet, whenever they stopped by, which she knew would be soon. She made him promise not to tell anyone where she was going. Back in the room, she sat with the paper on her lap:

To Janet,

My best friend, I'm sorry I lied to you; I wish I could go back and change things, so you wouldn't hate me. I love you.

To Daddy, Darren and Grandma,

I'm sorry, and I know you are ashamed of me, but I never meant to hurt any of you. Maybe someday I'll come back, and you can learn to forgive me. Grandma don't worry, I'll be fine where I'm going. I Love you.

To Rose,

I hope you forgive me, but if you truly love me like you say, then you'll understand why I had to leave this way. I hope you find the courage to live as your true self; you are too amazing to live as anything else. Don't bother looking for me; just know that I will be all right.

She folded up the notes and sat them on the table, before grabbing the necklace, her father's watch, the book, and turning out the light.

It was eight o'clock at night when they left. Christopher closed the store, while Darlene waited in the car. She thought about Rose and how heartbroken she would be when she came by to find her gone. She didn't want things to end this way, and she truly did care for Rose, but there was no other way. It was easier to leave without really having to say goodbye.

Darlene was quiet for most of the drive. She had too many thoughts going through her mind to engage in conversation.

"I don't know how I'll ever repay you." She told Christopher.

"You don't have to, but I hope you do come back. Someday. For your family, I mean."

He never had the courage to tell Darlene that he had always been attracted to her, but it didn't matter now. She was going through too much, and the last thing she would want to hear about is a silly crush. He also didn't want her to think that his attraction to her was the only reason he was helping. If anything, he hated to see her go just as the others would.

Darlene thought about what he said about returning to Durham someday—cooking with Grandma Anne again while they sang her favorite song, joking around with Darren, spending time with her father, and gossiping and playing hopscotch with Janet. Maybe even being with Rose again.

"Maybe," she replied, before laying her head against the window, and dozing off to sleep.

EPILOUGE

EIGHT YEARS LATER...

After leaving Durham to work for Christopher's uncle in Asheville, Darlene stayed on the farm for two years, working as a maid, maintaining the house. It wasn't much money, but she had a place to sleep and food to eat. She thought about going back home plenty of times but didn't know how she could look anyone in the face after what happened, or if anyone would even have her back.

In those two years, she saw Christopher twice—once when he and Muriel came by to visit during summer, and again for Hanukkah. He gave her updates on her family. After giving them the notes, Janet didn't say anything, but Grandma Anne cried. He hadn't seen her father, so he couldn't give any information on him. Rose had come by the next day after she left and was devastated. Christopher told Darlene that Rose demanded that he tell her where she went, but he refused. She came by the store every day for a week, then once a week for a while, until he never saw her again.

While in Asheville, Darlene met Luther Denton. He ran a blacksmith shop near the place she picked up groceries for Christopher's uncle. Being with Luther was new for her. She had never had a boyfriend before, and as far as having romantic feelings for anyone, Rose was the only person. She was never sure about how she felt about men until she met Luther. He was smart, kind, hardworking, and although he was a Christian, he was also a realist. He never let his faith in God cloud his judgement of others, and that was Darlene's favorite thing about him. He courted her for two months before asking for her hand in marriage. Shortly afterward, they moved to Roanoke, Virginia. He continued working as a blacksmith while Darlene finished school. Luther wanted a family, but Darlene swore to herself that after dropping out when she left Durham, that she had to go back to school and finish before she started a family. She became pregnant at twenty but suffered a miscarriage. After that, she wanted to wait a while before trying again. Now, at twenty-four, they were again expecting a child.

It was a Saturday morning when she got a letter in the mail. It was from Christopher. She had given him her address, so they could keep in touch when she moved away, since he was her only connection to her family. In the letter, he told her that her father had passed away of a heart attack. Darlene knew it was time. Luther knew she had family in Durham, but she told him they hadn't spoken in years. She showed him the letter and told him she'd be catching a train to North Carolina for her father's funeral. When she got back to Durham, it was as if she had never left. Everything looked the same. At the funeral, she saw Grandma Anne and Darren who was now married with three children of his own. He hugged his sister, rubbing her second- trimester belly, but didn't say much else to her. Grandma Anne was so happy to see Darlene she couldn't stop crying. She also saw Janet and Walter, who were now married to each other, with a daughter. Janet told her that she never hated her; she missed her and was glad to see her again after so many years. Her grandmother told her that her father never spoke of Darlene after that night at the house, but he always loved her. Despite his pride not allowing him to show it. Coming to his funeral to say goodbye and see him one last time resting in peace, was the closure Darlene needed.

After the service, she went back to her old house with Grandma Anne. Her grandmother gave her a box she had retrieved from Darlene's old bedroom. In the box were envelopes addressed to her from Rose. She couldn't believe her eyes. Her grandmother had secretly kept them hidden when her father wanted to throw them away. Darlene hadn't thought about Rose in a long time. She still had the necklace, sitting in a jewelry box inside her closet at home. She stopped wearing it once she married Luther. As she looked through the envelopes, they were all from an in-state residence, except for one. She opened them up one by one, reading them all. Most filled with hurt and apologies. The last few letters seemed calmer, wishing Darlene the best of luck wherever she was. Darlene assumed that writing these were Rose's way of healing, even if she never got a response. Darlene threw away all the letters after reading but kept one of the envelopes written three years earlier. It was from New York City.

Back home in Roanoke, she decided to write back. It was a long shot, and there was no guarantee Rose still lived at this address, but it was worth a shot. A few weeks later, she got a response. Rose was still living in New York City. She was thrilled to hear from her and wanted to come to Virginia to see her. Darlene was skeptic, but after a month of contemplating, she finally wrote back saying it was okay. After eight years, the girls would finally see each other again. Rose drove to Virginia a few weeks later, and Darlene invited her to have dinner with her and Luther. She introduced Rose as a friend from Durham. She never lied to her husband, but also knew it was better not to share some details. After dinner, Rose and Darlene went outside to sit in Darlene's garden in the back yard. Rose told her that after Darlene left, she had come out to her parents. It didn't go well, so she took it upon herself to leave. She took her trust fund and left town.

Three years ago, she moved to New York City. Mr. and Mrs. Caldwell came to visit her once since she left. They told her that she could come back home if she gave up her lesbian lifestyle, but of course, she refused. She hasn't seen them since, but she writes often, even though they never write back. She was currently dating a woman named Bonnie. They met not too long after Rose moved to New York and Bonnie was a waitress at the time. She introduced Rose to the low-profile gay scene, which inspired her to open a speakeasy for lesbian women called Over the Rainbow. Her trust fund money was enough to purchase the building, where she and Bonnie ran the business together. The two women talked for hours, and promised they would keep in touch, as friends and nothing more. Hearing Rose talk about Bonnie the way she used to talk about her made Darlene happy. She was glad Rose could move on and find someone who seemed perfect for her. Darlene thought that maybe in another time, where things were different, it could've been her. But it was all in the past now, and just knowing that someone she once cared about was alive and well, living her best life, was enough. They had each other, but in a different way now. Darlene plucked one of her carnations and held it up to her nose.

This is what true happiness smells like.

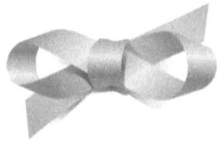

Quotes from famous LGBTQ icons from the past and present.

"LOVE HIM AND LET HIM love you. Do you think anything else under heaven really matters?" -James Baldwin

• • ∞ • •

"IF A TRANSVESTITE DOESN'T say I'm gay and I'm proud and I'm a transvestite, then nobody else is going to hop up there and say I'm gay and I'm proud and I'm a transvestite for them."
– Marsha P. Johnson

• • ∞ • •

"SOME OF US WEAR THE symbols and badges of our non-conformity." -Gladys Bentley

• • ∞ • •

"MY ACTIVISM DID NOT spring from my being gay, or, for that matter, from my being black. Rather, it is rooted fundamentally in my Quaker upbringing and the values that were instilled in me by my grandparents who reared me."
-Bayard Rustin

• • ∞ • •

"IT WAS A REBELLION, it was an uprising, it was a civil rights disobedience, it wasn't no damn riot" -Stormé DeLarverie

• • ∞ • •

"I HAVE COME TO BELIEVE over and over again that what is most important to me must be spoken, made verbal and shared, even at the risk of having it bruised or misunderstood." -Audre Lorde

. . ᘓ . .

"DELIVER ME FROM WRITERS who say the way they live doesn't matter. I'm not sure a bad person can write a good book, If art doesn't make us better, then what on earth is it for." -Alice Walker

. . ᘓ . .

"BROADWAY! BROAD-WAY! I don't aspire to the middle. I aspire to the tip-tip-top of it all." -Billy Porter

. . ᘓ . .

"WE ARE A PEOPLE IN a quandary about the present. We are a people in search of our future. We are a people in search of a national community." -Barbara Jordan

. . ᘓ . .

"YOU HAVE TO PAY ATTENTION to the moment and make it the best it can be for you. I've been trying to do that. It's really made a major difference for me. I'm a happier person." -Tracy Chapman

. . ᘓ . .

"WHEN YOU PUT LOVE OUT in the world it travels, and it can touch people and reach people in ways that we never even expected." -Laverne Cox

. . ᘓ . .

"MY HEART KNOWS WHO i am and who i'll turn out to be!" -E. Lynn Harris

. . ҈ . .

"THE IDEA OF FREEDOM is inspiring. But what does it mean? If you are free in a political sense but have no food, what's that? The freedom to starve?" -Angela Davis

. . ҈ . .

"I THINK EVERYTHING should happen at halfway to dawn. That's when all the heads of government should meet. I think everybody would fall in love." -Billy Strayhorn

. . ҈ . .

"LOOK AT PEOPLE FOR an example, but then make sure to do things your way. Surround yourself with positive people." -Queen Latifah

. . ҈ . .

"WHEN I'M AROUND PEOPLE having conversations about their day, I'm looking at them, like, 'What could they possibly be talking about? How are we not talking about deconstructing white supremacy right now? How are we not trying to save trans people?" -Indya Moore

. . ҈ . .

"I FEEL LIKE HARRIET Tubman, except I am trying to free people through underground music, to free themselves creatively and inspirationally." - Janelle Monae

. . ҈ . .

"I WASN'T REALLY NAKED. I simply didn't have any clothes on." -Josephine Baker

. . ҈ . .

"THOUGH IT BE A THRILLING and marvelous thing to be merely young and gifted in such times, it is doubly so - doubly dynamic - to be young, gifted and black." -Lorraine Hansberry

. . ✿ . .

"I NEED A LITTLE SUGAR in my bowl and a little hot dog in my roll." -Bessie Smith

. . ✿ . .

"IF A TRANS WOMAN WHO knows herself and operates in the world as a woman is seen, perceived, treated, and viewed as a woman, isn't she just being herself? She isn't passing; she is merely being." -Janet Mock

Check out other books by Chanel

Fernando
Was It Her?
Mahogany Tales
P.S. I Hope This Finds You
The Moonlight Series
Delicate: A Collection of poems
I Had a Dream About You: A Collection of Poems
Sweet Oleander: A Collection of Poetry

About the Publisher